# THE CARVED ANGEL

# The Carved Angel

## John Hutchins

With Illustrations
by Jane Andrew

UNITED WRITERS
Cornwall

UNITED WRITERS PUBLICATIONS LTD
Ailsa, Castle Gate, Penzance, Cornwall.
www.unitedwriters.co.uk

British Library Cataloguing in Publication Data:
A catalogue record for this book is
available from the British Library.

ISBN 9781852001711

Printed and bound in Great Britain by
United Writers Publications Ltd.,
Cornwall.

*To my 'beloved Ma' – my mother Doris
for all her continued
love, support and friendship.*

# Acknowledgements

There are many people I'd like to thank who helped me on the journey to complete this, my first (and hopefully not my last) novel, although there are too many to mention here. For those not listed, please forgive me.

The first is my friend, fellow United Writers' author and *Tavistock Times Gazette* co-worker Ted Sherrell, to whom I am indebted for his wise words and guidance. This book would perhaps not have been completed without his encouragement.

*The Carved Angel* has been much enhanced with the excellent drawings by my friend, Jane Andrew, a former colleague on the *Falmouth Packet* and *West Briton* newspapers in Cornwall. Jane has, through the skill of her pencil, helped bring scenes from the story to life and the book has been much enriched by her artistic talents.

I am also indebted to fellow members of the Plymouth Athenaeum Writers' Group, who have patiently heard extracts from the book on many a Monday evening and provided me with constructive criticism and encouragement.

A great big thank you to publisher Malcolm Sheppard of United Writers for giving me the opportunity and for finding the time to ensure *The Carved Angel* is published at such a momentous time – 100 years since the outbreak of the First World War.

Many thanks to Jonathan Kindleysides, the assistant keeper of mining life at the excellent Beamish Open Air Museum in County Durham. Jonathan kindly read the mining chapters and gave much valued advice in my attempts to provide some authenticity in writing about life down the pits just before the First World War.

Finally to my grandfathers, Joseph Ruby and William Hutchins, whose lives were forever touched by The Great War.

# Chapter One

*April 1920:*

'Right oh, Mr Parkman, sir, no trouble,' said the gravedigger.

'Make sure you do it today, Tommy; vicar won't like it if you get behind,' the verger replied.

'Aye, Mr Parkman, sir,' said Tommy. 'It will be done.'

Tommy touched his cap, picked up his shovel and headed for plot 319. He marked out the grave with the sharp end of the shovel, and when he was satisfied with the length and breadth he began to dig. His foot hit the shoulder of the steel blade and the earth parted.

'I like digging,' thought Tommy. 'Hard graft, honest toil, fresh air. I like digging.'

While he was labouring away he heard the distant clip clop of horses' hooves on the cobbled stones gradually becoming louder until they stopped outside the entrance to the graveyard. Four carriages full of mourners began to form an orderly queue respectfully outside St Anthony the Abbot in the North Riding town of Yeasley.

'Another customer,' sighed Tommy. He paused, respectfully took off his cap, and once the cortège had passed was about to return to his labours.

Then a tall, well-built man in his early thirties carried a casket in his arms containing the body of a little four-year-old girl. Tommy looked into the face of the big fellow. It was as if the man's eyes shone no light, but as he passed plot 319 the gravedigger could see a tear trickle down the cheek of his strong, chiselled face.

Behind the man, who Tommy assumed to be the infant's father, was a small, attractive woman, slightly stooped by her grief as she followed her husband and dead child. The woman sobbed as she shuffled towards the grave. In her hands she grasped tight a small teddy bear, which had a button black nose with amber and black glass eyes and a coat of dirty brown – no doubt once a beloved favourite of her now dead daughter. The young mother, dressed immaculately all in black, appeared unaware of those around and locked into her own world of personal grief. The sombre expressions of those who followed the grieving parents only added to the distressing scene.

As the party congregated around the freshly dug grave Tommy continued with his work. With his big hands wrapped around the handle of the shovel he quickly got into his rhythm of scooping the soil out of the ground and soon there was a large heap of earth beside plot 319.

Deep in their grief, and crowded around the burial pit with their backs to Tommy, the mourners took no notice as the gravedigger, from a distance, continued his work, despite the fresh wind and heavy drizzle.

As the rain fell, some of the mourners raised an umbrella for protection and Reverend Collins performed the latest Christian burial at St Anthony's.

Women sobbed openly and men looked down feeling helpless – wondering at the cruelty of a world where the life of a sweet, innocent four-year-old is cut so tragically short.

The young woman stepped forward and, as the casket was slowly lowered into the ground, she carefully placed the little bear on top of the tiny wooden box. She blew a farewell kiss and whispered a choked goodbye to her little girl before it all became too much for her to endure. Her husband, trying hard himself to control his own shattered emotions, stepped forward, wrapped his arms around his wife, and lovingly dragged her away, despite her cries of woe which pierced the hearts of all those around her.

Tommy momentarily stopped his digging and looked at the pitiful scene. He mouthed, although nobody heard him, 'God bless,' both to the little girl and her grieving parents. He stood erect, just for a few seconds, before turning away and resuming his digging. Indeed, while he dug Tommy soon had other things on his mind. Every shovel full of soil he extracted from the rich Northern earth only served to dig his thoughts even deeper from the present.

# Chapter Two

*August 1912:*

'Put you back into it lad,' said Da with a smile on his face. 'Yer 'av to learn 'ow to dig like a collier.'

Tommy, aged 14, thrust the spade into the stony soil but the spade bounced back and he felt a discomforting tingle shoot up his arm. Victor, 13, and Edward, 12, stood watching beside him and grinned. They would rather be kicking a football or having a fight with the Mooney twins than watch their eldest brother digging.

'Come on, Tommy, show your brothers 'ow it's done. 'Ow we going to grow any tatties if you can't even scratch the soil,' reproached Da, though with a kindly taunt.

The remark just doubled Tommy's resolve, making him more determined to show his brothers he was capable of 'men's work' as well as to impress his Da.

Despite the younger ones' apparent boredom the boys really liked going to the allotment with Da because it was one of the few precious times they spent together, as he was either too tired or too ill after spending the week working down the pit. It was also a way, they all knew, of helping Ma and Da put 'food on the table'.

Ma used to say any food from the 'patch', as she called the allotment, helped to 'keep the wolf from the door', to which Victor once quipped 'that it must be workin' cuz he hadn't seen any wolves in Hillthorpe for ages.' Even Da laughed at that one.

All the families in the village had a claim to a piece of the allotment. The land was subsidised by the colliers' union who rented it off the mine owners. The owners 'consented' to lease it to union members as they wished to be seen as 'enlightened employers' – caring for the welfare of their workers, although in reality the land was useless for anything else and this way would bring them in an income.

After their Sunday afternoon in the patch was over the males of the Wagstaff clan returned to the house. Ma was in the kitchen, dressed in her only apron, preparing the evening meal by rolling out the pastry for a 'tattie pie'. Ten-year-old Emma was standing by her side, sprinkling the flour on Ma's instruction. They both smiled on seeing all 'their boys' return to the family home.

Following their supper Da began to do what he did on many an evening, and started to whittle. While Ma and the children carried on with the washing up and clearing the utensils, he loved working the wood into little figures. Over the years Da used his skill to make many toys for the children.

He had picked up a discarded small piece of pine from the mine tunnel floor and over the past few evenings had skilfully carved out a little figurine.

Da would never let anyone see his carving until he had finished it although little Emma had sneaked a look and was most impressed; with her eleventh birthday only a few days away she was hoping that Da's latest figurine was for her.

Da sat with his back to the children and whittled away, only stopping now and again when a bout of his hacking cough took hold and he would rasp his throat before disgorging the resulting contents into a spittoon – always away from the children.

Once he was satisfied with this 'secret carving' he smiled at Ma. He wrapped it up in a little cloth and for the rest of the

14

evening proceeded to rub the figurine until he was satisfied that all its surfaces were smooth. Da then took out his 'special pot' of linseed oil, which he had traded with Jimmy Firman, the pit's master carpenter, for one of his homing pigeons. He then rubbed the precious oil into the carved pine to let it soak into its pores.

Once it was finished Ma and Da went outside for a 'bit of Ma and Da time', as they called it, while the children entertained themselves in the parlour.

The parents soon returned and immediately there was silence.

'Tommy,' said Ma, 'we have a little present for you, since you start down the pit tomorrow.'

With that she unwrapped from the oil-stained rag a shiny, carved wooden angel, complete with feathered wings and holding its arms out in a protective embrace.

'It's so beautiful,' cooed little Emma, but with more than a hint of disappointment in her young voice.

Ma sensed her sadness.

'Now, our Emma,' she said, 'I know you had your eye on Da's carving but don't you fret lass; Da's promised to make you one too, and later on for Edward and Victor – haven't you Da?'

Da nodded.

'This one's especially for our Tommy, to protect him wherever he goes and particularly down the pits. This angel represents St Barbara, the patron saint of miners. Now you want your brother to be safe and under her protection down there, don't you Emma?' asked Ma.

Emma smiled: ' 'Course I do Ma,' she said, and she took it from her and passed the angel to Tommy.

'You take it Tommy,' said Emma. 'Look after the angel and the angel will look after you. I know it will.'

With that she wrapped her arms around her big brother's waist and gave him a hug.

'Thanks Da. Thanks Ma,' said Tommy, not without a little embarrassment in front of Victor and Edward.

'Thanks Emma. I'll look after it, I promise,' and with that he sat down and stared at the little figurine for a while before putting it into his pocket.

Although he never said it at the time, he didn't have the same confidence as Ma and Emma over the powers of the little carved angel which, to him, was just a piece of shapen wood, discarded from a pit prop. However, Tommy knew he would treasure it as long as he lived because it was made lovingly by his Da, blessed by his Ma and 'given' to him by his little sis. From that moment, wherever he went so did the little pine angel.

# Chapter Three

By the age of 12 most of the boys at Hillthorpe Elementary School left to join their fathers, elder brothers and uncles to work at the colliery.

Tommy was lucky, said his da, who on constant occasions reminded him that, 'I wuz only 11 when I had to take a job in the screens to bring money to the table.'

Only two boys avoided this annual 'cull' as some local wit had named it – one Ronald Dawson, who was the 'top boy' in his class and went to Gigthorpe Grammar School, eight miles away, to further his education, thanks considerably to a scholarship provided from funds of the North Yorkshire and Durham Miners' Union. The other beneficiary was Cedric Swanton, whose parents – one of only three Catholic families in the village – sent him to prepare for college at St Bede's seminary at Wallsend and a life in the priesthood.

Although the boys had been brought up around the mine, had it 'in their blood' and breathed it in their very nostrils daily, it was still a shock to the latest batch of 'pit bairns' – as they were called by the colliers – to be introduced to the underworld that was to be their future, and for many, 'til the day they died.

From the ages of 12 to 14, they worked in the screens – the

17

sorting sheds – separating the pieces of coal by grade and size. The boys worked under some of the older colliers – those, due to their age or infirmity, who were no longer able to meet the physical demands of the coal face.

As one old timer, Luke Shortcross, told Tommy: 'You start yer pit life in the screens and you end yer pit life in the screens.'

Tommy was not too impressed by the thought.

For two years Tommy continued with this work, not complaining and 'doin' as ee wuz told'. It held little fascination for him but he took pride that he was now helping Ma and Da with a wage, albeit a small one.

One thing he didn't want though, was to end up like Luke Shortcross and be a miner all his life – although Tommy didn't really know if there was much choice open to him.

One early November morning the boys were told to go to the pithead and wait for further instruction.

Sixteen new, if not all eager, pit bairns gathered at the colliery head. It was cold, dark and 5.50am with the wind and rain adding to their discomfort. Some of the lads looked as white as a sheet at the prospect of 'goin' down' but none of them even tried to convey their true feelings, which were really a mixture of excitement and fear. Two of the 'tougher lads' tried to give the impression to the others that it was something they had done many times before, having gone down with their das and brothers – something that was strictly against the company rules.

Tommy and the rest of the boys were greeted by 'Old Saul', a friendly collier who, sensing the boys' apprehension, tried to put them at ease.

'Don't worry, lads. You might be freezing up 'ere but you'll soon warm up.'

Whether this had the desired effect on the fresh intake was hard to fathom – one or two of the lads took a distinctive turn for the worse.

'I hope it ain't too warm,' piped up the cheeky Bert Dyson. 'My brother Stanley said it's hot as Hell itself down there.'

18

That brought a smile to the face of Old Saul and most of the other boys but it was a bit too near the knuckle for Nobby Blaydon, who responded to Bert's image and turned away to throw up the porridge his Ma had just given him twenty minutes earlier for breakfast.

All the boys were issued with a Davy lamp and a small, metal named disc to help those at the surface to ascertain who were down the pit at any one time. The latter they gave to the 'tally man' who operated the 'cage', whose lift took them 350 feet down the shaft into the mine itself.

Tommy and the other boys crammed into the metal cage. Once they were in, Old Saul tapped the bars, the tally man pulled a lever, the cage jerked, the winding gear began to operate and the occupants slowly descended into the pit.

'Don't worry, lads,' encouraged Old Saul again. 'Yer soon get used to it. Takes you eyes a little time to get used to the dark, but you will. Yer be all right, boys.'

As soon as they hit the pit floor level, the cage was opened by Old Saul and the boys pushed forward anxiously into the darkness. The collier raised his lamp so everyone could see his face. The heat of the mine and the foetid atmosphere was the first sensation the boys felt, that and the rumbling noise of the coal wagons on the metal rail tracks and the distinctive tapping of colliers picking at the seam in the near distance.

'Now lads,' said Old Saul: 'Do as you are told and no going wunderin'. Mines are dangerous places, so keep your ears open, your eyes sharp and your noses sniffin'. Keep the caps on your lamps closed. Naked flames can cause explosions, so no naked flames, anytime. You've been told a hundred times.'

'Two hundred and fifty,' shouted Bert and all the boys laughed.

'Yer job,' continued an unruffled Old Saul, 'is to push the carts, both the empties and the full ones, up and down the seam. Watch out, they are heavy and if they catch you, most of you being skin and bone, they can do you serious damage.'

'So lads, be careful and. . .' before he could finish the boys shouted in chorused unison, 'No naked flames.'

Tommy soon found himself teaming up with Bert. After a couple of shifts they became friends. Tommy learned that Bert was from the nearby village of Daleswick and had joined the Hillthorpe boys as his home pit had not taken on so many 'apprentices' that year.

One of the lads with Tommy was his 'old' pal Walter Smethick, known to his friends and family as 'Wally'.

There wasn't much of Walter Smethick, 5ft 2ins and barely eight and a half stone soaking wet, but beware any boy in Hillthorpe who got on the wrong side of him; for an avowed pacifist he packed a mean right hook! Tommy had a great liking for his mate Wally. He was in the same class at the village school and they sat next to each other for four years.

He remembered they shared the same desk – not unusual as all the other pupils in Hillthorpe Elementary School had to do the same because there weren't enough desks to go around. Young Tommy knew he had found a friend the moment Mr Neilsen, the teacher, commanded Wally to 'sit up straight and stop slouching in his chair.'

'Sorry sir,' replied Wally in an instant. 'I was only copying you. I won't do it again.'

The whole class erupted in laughter but not the stern faced, humourless Mr Neilsen. Tommy thought it was a bit harsh when the rather miffed teacher decided to give Wally 'six of the best' with his hickory cane, but admired the way the boy took his punishment in silence.

In the playground Wally was just as dogmatic. When all the boys lined up to have a big scrap, Wally just sat on the wall and refused to join in.

Harold Jenkinson made the mistake of mocking Wally and calling him 'a big girl's blouse' – the ultimate insult to a then eight-year-old boy.

Wally jumped down from the wall, marched directly up to Harold and grabbed him by the throat. Even though the 'victim' of the jugular assault was five inches taller and at least twenty pounds heavier, it did not stop his assailant grabbing his windpipe and extracting any air left in the unfortunate boy's body.

'My da is a Christian Pacifist and says all fighting is evil and we must not fight each other.'

These words were of little comfort to Harold, who, owing to a lack of oxygen, began to turn a distinct shade of blue.

'My da said that if he ever catches even a whiff of me fightin' 'e will beat the livin' daylights out of me,' continued Wally with his knee firmly pinned in Harold's groin.

Harold was grateful that the message was relayed, as he slid down the wall and gasped desperately to suck air into his deflated lungs.

'He certainly knows 'ow to get his point across, does our Wally,' thought Tommy.

# Chapter Four

During the next few months the boys began to adjust to the routine of life down the mine, pulling and pushing the heavy carts, running errands for the colliers and, most importantly of all, leaving proudly each Friday, a couple of shillings – their whole wage packet – to their Mas on the kitchen table.

Old Saul continued to keep an eye on Tommy and Bert, as he indeed did on all the lads, although he had no trouble with these two 'pit bairns' – he even gave them the odd toffee sweet he had concealed in his numerous pockets, or a slice of apple at break time.

The boys liked the man who treated them well – far better than their old teachers, who were not adverse to wielding their canes for the slightest misdemeanour on many an occasion.

'How old is Old Saul, you reckon Bert?' asked Tommy.

'He must be in his thirties at least Tommy,' he answered, before adding, 'Wally Smethick heard he was forty-two.'

'That's very old,' said Tommy.

It was indeed hard to determine Old Saul's real age, not helped by the fact that he had a crooked back, caused through a cave-in twelve years before, and the ever informed Bert said it was known he suffered badly with 'joint trouble', which meant he could no longer dig like other and younger colliers. Like many of the miners, Old Saul walked with bandy legs, brought about by working in confined tunnels with low ceilings for years and being forced to 'duck his head' and amble, crab like, along the pit face.

Nevertheless, Tommy and Bert respected and looked up to the man who, to them, at least they could talk to – the other miners were so wrapped up in their own work as they were only paid for what they produced per ton, that they had no time for 'pit bairns.' Unless, of course, they got in the way; and woe betide any boy who did, because they could expect, and received, an instant lash of the tongue or a painful clip on the ear if they did.

One morning Tommy and Bert were leaning on the back of a cart, talking about how Newcastle United were going to do against Aston Villa on Saturday at St James' Park and dreaming if they would be allowed to go and see their favourite football team one day.

All of a sudden they heard the distinctive click, click, click of a coal cart heading towards them along the rail line and, before they had time to react, they were jolted through the air violently onto the ground after their half full cart was smashed into at speed by an out of control wagon. Once they recovered from the shock, Tommy and Bert picked themselves up, dusted themselves down and checked if there was any bleeding or bruising.

They looked up and saw Archie Tilsley, hanging on the back of the offending truck and laughing at their 'accident'. Both the victims glared back in anger at his sheer stupidity.

Tilsley jumped down from the truck he had been recklessly riding – purposely pushing it to the limit to gain the maximum speed before the resulting impact with his intended target.

Bert could not contain his wrath.

'You bleedin' idiot, you could have killed us, Tilsley,' he blurted.

'Stop whinin' you little shite,' replied the older boy. 'You wuz waggin' like a couple of Whitby fishwives. Now get on with yer work before I punch your lights out.'

'Don't tell me what to do, Tilsley,' snarled Bert, clearly incensed and, despite being a good couple of stones and four inches shorter than his adversary, certainly ready to turn Tilsley's 'lights out' first.

Tommy instinctively stepped in between the two antagonists and Tilsley took a step back when the bigger of the friends intervened.

'What's going on down there?' came a voice. It was Old Saul who heard the clatter from more than a 100 yards away and came running, or more accurately hobbling, to the scene fearing the worst.

'These pit bairns have spilled over a cart, Saul,' said Tilsley. 'Larking about, if you ask me. Young uns, eh? He added, and tutted in disgust for effect. The seventeen-year-old collier was hoping that Old Saul would share his distain of such youthful pranks.

But Old Saul was not fooled.

'Get back to your work place, Tilsley. Not that yer mates will be missing you,' he said, looking him straight in the eye. 'I thought you might be involved. Now go and report to the foreman, I'm sure he'll find you some real work instead of just larking about.'

'I've dug more coal this week than you, you old cripple,' snarled Tilsley, and with that he turned, sniggering to himself, and headed back to 'work'.

'Ee, 'ee's a bad un,' exclaimed Old Saul, rubbing the back of his head. 'No good will come of 'im, I tell ee.'

Old Saul looked at Tommy and Bert.

'You alreet lads?' he inquired.

They nodded, and Old Saul helped them righten the cart that was tipped over and began to shovel its disgorged contents back in before leaving them, to return to his duties.

Bert explained to Tommy that Archie Tilsley came from the same village as him. Tilsley used to work in the coal pit there but none of the colliers liked the 'cocky little waster' and he soon lost his job when the foreman got fed up with his 'doin's'.

'The Tilsleys are a bad bunch and 'e's the worst,' added Bert.

'He tried to steal my da's coal share once when they were ganged up, claiming it was his after stealin' it from Da's cart. My Da smacked him and wuz laid off for two days and lost his pay for fightin'. Since then the Tilsleys 'av always caused us trouble when they can.

Tommy nodded and sensed that this was not to be his last meeting with Archie Tilsley.

Indeed, it was not long before he witnessed another unfortunate incident involving the 'black sheep of Daleswick'.

If there was one instruction that was drilled into a miner from his very first day it was the absolute taboo on smoking underground at any time!

The danger of explosions from a single spark igniting the coal dust and the gas that permeated the air was a constant threat. There was not a mine in North Yorkshire, or in the whole of the North East, that not had its own tale of such a disaster.

Archie Tilsley liked his 'baccy' – he had been smoking it since the age of eleven – and he was not alone among his fellow colliers; but the difference between him and his fellow colliers was that they were not so reckless or foolhardy and knew when to heed the rules for the sake of everybody's safety and well being.

It was the policy of the management, for both economic reasons and the welfare of their employees, that any man or boy going underground was searched for matches and cigarettes. If anyone was caught it was instant dismissal, because one spark from an errant match could cause the deaths of scores or even hundreds and endanger the whole mine.

However, Tilsley was a temperamental teenager and not the sort to heed sensible advice, certainly from the likes of Old Saul and his ilk. 'Rules' were there to be broken and only served, in Archie Tilsley, to provoke a challenge against authority. He soon found a way to smuggle the banned 'smokies', as he called them, by concealing his stash on his person. He hollowed out his laces and stuffed them with matches while the tobacco was hidden in

25

his lamp. Once down in the mine he then hid them both in a dry storage place unknown to anyone but himself.

Young Tilsley thought to himself that he knew when to have a crafty fag or not, so no harm would be done.

'Why, he had been down the pits for three years now and was an experienced collier,' he reasoned. He wasn't as stupid as the other lads, and besides, he knew where it was and wasn't safe to have a quick puff – all he needed was his Davy lamp and his instincts.

So after one particularly hard grafting shift – hard grafting for the other men in his gang, at least – Tilsley decided he deserved the reward of a 'rolly'. Tucked discreetly behind a protruding pit prop so no one could see him, he began, expertly, his well practised rolling of the tobacco shag into the tapered thin paper. He stood up, stuck the finished cigarette into his mouth and was just about to strike a Swan Vesta match to light its tip.

Just at that moment Jethro Toon, the shot man, came around the corner with Tommy, who that morning was charged with carrying the box of detonators for Jethro's next controlled explosion.

When Jethro, who was an amateur boxer and in the words of his fellow colliers 'not a man to be messed with', saw Tilsley about to light up, he himself lit up with rage.

Within less than the flick of an eyelid, and before Tilsley could complete the strike, Toon knocked the match out of his hand with his right fist.

'You bloody stupid wassock,' boomed Toon. 'You could have us all killed!'

Tilsley looked at him first with astonishment, surprised that he had been discovered, but secondly with annoyance when realising he just lost a decent cigarette.

He started to voice his protest, but before Tilsley could utter a syllable the irate Toon, a southpaw, smacked the wretched youth with the force that any drill hammer would have been proud of. The punch propelled Tilsley at a rate of knots into the pit wall and

26

blood came oozing out of his mouth, dribbling down his chin before he spat out a couple of teeth.

'That, boy, is so you remember a lesson,' boomed Toon, who stood over the crumbled heap of Tilsley sprawled on the deck. He grabbed the front of Tilsley's shirt with one hand so his face was level with his object of scorn. Pointing an accusing finger and looking at Tilsley straight in the eye, Toon slowly, but in words which would leave no room for discussion, declared: 'If you ever do that again, boy, yer soft headed little runt, I will kill yer.' And there was nobody in the pits and for miles around who had the slightest doubt that Jethro Toon was a man of his word.

Tommy looked at Tilsley, who was on the deck almost quivering with shock after his 'confrontation' with Toon and rubbing his jaw to make sure it was all in one piece.

'I'll be reporting this to the gaffer,' added Toon. 'If you want to make a complaint be my guest.'

Toon then nodded to Tommy, signalling him to follow him to continue their work.

Once he had gained some sense of composure, the humiliated Tilsley glared up at Toon, though not daring to look him in the eye and his gaze soon moved to Tommy; but Tommy was wise enough not to return it and followed the shot man up the coal face.

There is an old adage that 'old dogs cannot learn new tricks' – in Archie Tilsley's case it was more one of a young dog refusing to learn old ones.

# Chapter Five

Just six weeks after that incident, Tommy and Bert were working the carts at the entrance of 'Dame Nellie'. The colliers liked to think the latest new seam of coal was a 'lucky' one and in a rare moment of sentiment always named it after something they mutually loved.

One set of three seams were named Veitch, McCracken and Rutherford after the colliers' Newcastle United footballing heroes.

As another shared passion was music 'Dame Nellie Melba' was another named seam along with 'Jenny Lind' and 'Marie Lloyd' – musical stars who not one man in the pit had ever seen, let alone heard.

Dame Nellie was an old seam, more than twenty years old, but the coal surveyor and mine manager decided to take some samples to see if 'a more modern scientific approach' since its closure may yield fresh dividends if it was reopened. So, in preparation for this new survey, the wooden boarded entrance to Dame Nellie was taken down and work had already begun by some of the colliers to replace old buttresses and put in new props.

Among those doing the labour was Old Saul, who had Tommy

by his side, and a couple of experienced men – Godwin Bullock and Peter Dovecote – along with an amiable, hard working lad called Joe Sydon, who was just a year older than Tommy. Joe's Da was a good friend of Tommy's Da, who had both worked together for years in the same pit and shared an interest in homing pigeons.

The site foreman, Sid Jessop, had taken the precaution to check Dame Nellie for methane gas. Methane, or 'firedamp' as the miners knew it, was a potentially deadly gas if it built up in huge quantities, something it tended to do, especially in old workings; however, initial surveys showed that although there were traces in the air it was not large enough to be thought dangerous and work was allowed to continue.

The work party were in good spirits and productive in their work and if progress advanced at the same rate, reckoned Old Saul, then Dame Nellie could be reopened as early as next week.

Sid Jessop came up the tunnel, followed by three men, one of whom was Tilsley.

'Mornin' Saul, three more to give you a hand,' said the foreman.

Old Saul turned around slowly, lowered a lump hammer he was working with, and welcomed Jessop with a smile, tugging his cap in respect.

'Thank ye gaffer, they'll be handy,' said Old Saul.

For the next two hours things went smoothly and Old Saul called a halt so the men and boys could have a rest and a bottle of refreshment. Even Archie Tilsley, for once, appeared to be pulling his weight – though appearances could be deceptive. As soon as the order to 'down tools' was given Tilsley disappeared to the mouth of the tunnel.

He had his back to Bert when the latter came up the tunnel pushing a cart; it was Bert's job to take out any debris that the collier gang had extracted from Dame Nellie.

Bert, straining to push the cart which was heavy enough even if empty, noticed that Tilsley's back arched as he bowed his head;

hearing the clatter of the cart wheels Tilsley turned, surprised to see Bert behind him. In his hand was a freshly rolled up cigarette, now almost finished. Tilsley glared at Bert, not happy he had been seen. He inhaled deeply on the tab before exhaling with exaggerated satisfaction, as if this was supposed to impress Bert. Tilsley stared menacingly at Bert and gave him a sickly grin before flicking, with his finger and thumb, the remains of his dog-end back into the tunnel. Bert would never forget the look at that exact moment on Tilsley's face – it was nearly the last moment in his own short life.

The next thing Bert knew he was flying through the air backwards from the tunnel. There was an almighty ringing in his ears and coal dust filled his lungs and his eyes could not see for blackness.

The explosion had travelled up the tunnel with a mighty velocity, creating a blast that channelled through the confined space of its walls and ripped through the entire length of Dame Nellie.

Bert, who was thrown on to the ground, just missing the steel track lines, gasped for air. After what seemed an eternity, but was really less than a minute, he rubbed his eyes, cleared his throat and staggered to his feet.

With the draught going up the tunnel, the dust cloud eventually began to clear. Bert saw Tilsley on the floor, having been thrown against the wall of the pit, but conscious and groaning. Bert looked into the entrance of the tunnel and saw just a heap of rubble and huge slabs of coal.

'Tommy, Tommy,' he tried to scream, but the words could not get out of his mouth.

Fortunately, just before the blast Tommy had heard the rumble of the cart and knew that it was Bert pushing it, so instinctively went towards the entrance to greet him. It was an action that undoubtedly saved his life.

Despite the danger of further collapses from the roof of the tunnel, Bert ran into the abyss. He scampered over the debris and

31

made out an arm protruding from the rubble. He frantically dug around it and soon discovered it was his friend. Tommy was moaning in pain but he was alive. The only sensible words that Bert could make out were Tommy muttering, 'Saul, where's Old Saul?'

Somehow, with strength he did not know he possessed, Bert managed to excavate Tommy from the rubble. Just as he was dragging him out of the entrance he was joined by Tilsley, now recovered, who took Tommy's legs while Bert held his shoulders.

Around twenty colliers came running up to the tunnel entrance, most with picks and shovels, among them Sid Jessop and Wally Smethick. They arrived just as Bert and Tilsley were laying Tommy out on the ground.

'We got one of them out,' panted Tilsley. 'There's more in there.'

Sid Jessop ignored Tilsley and concentrated on a plan of action to rescue his fellow colliers.

He ordered three of the more experienced colliers to go into the tunnel and first make sure that it was safe from any more collapsing coal seams; once they had given the all clear he ordered the remainder, except Wally, to start digging to rescue those trapped.

Wally attended to Tommy who was bleeding from cuts to his head and arm; Wally proceeded to stem the flow of blood by ripping up his own shirt and making and applying bandages to his friend's wounds.

Gradually Tommy began to come round. 'Saul, where's Old Saul?' he pleaded, but Bert and Wally did not answer.

Wally glanced down at Tommy's side and saw the little carved angel figurine laying on the floor. It had tumbled out of Tommy's pocket as he was being cared for by his friend. Wally picked it up.

'It must be Tommy's good luck charm,' thought Wally, and put it in his trouser pocket for safekeeping before continuing to tend Tommy's wounds as best he could.

A full-scale rescue operation was soon in motion around them, one that the miners practised in their own spare time in case of such an eventuality.

Above the pit, news of the disaster soon spread and the continuing whines of the colliery hooter only added to the fear of every family in Hillthorpe. Soon hundreds of people were at the pit head waiting anxiously for news, boosted in numbers as more family members arrived by the minute from Daleswick.

Ma and Da Wagstaff, along with Victor, Edward and Emma, gathered half in shock, half in anticipation, for word about their Tommy. It was too much for little Emma who burst into tears, fearing the worst for her beloved brother, and she clung tightly to her mother for some sort of comfort.

Eventually the shaft lift was opened to bring up the men. Tommy was brought out supported under each shoulder by Fred Barker and Wally Smethick.

Emma ran over and put her arms around his waist; she was soon joined by Ma, who hugged him so tightly that Tommy winced with the pain from his bruised body.

'Tommy, Tommy, thank God. I prayed you'd be all right, Tom,' and she hugged and kissed him again in sheer relief, much to the embarrassment of Tommy, who reckoned the whole of the village was watching.

Wally reached in his pocket and, taking out the angel, briefly interrupted the family reunion.

'I found this next to you, Tommy, laying by your side,' he said and handed the angel back to him.

Emma gasped in delight. 'I told you, Tommy, the little angel would look after you.' She and Ma smiled at each other before Ma grabbed Tommy again and pulled him to her bosom.

But Ma soon let go of Tommy when she saw the stretcher bearers carrying out the corpses; the bodies covered completely by blankets. As the rest of the miners came up in the cages, although their faces were blackened, their features looked pallid and lifeless.

There were cries of anguish from relatives when the names of the dead were broken to the crowd – Old Saul, Godwin Bullock, Peter Dovecote and little Joe Sydon.

The last cage to come to the surface contained about ten miners – among them Sid Jessop, and behind him Bert Dyson and Archie Tilsley. Sid Jessop had a face like thunder.

He was greeted by Sgt Milburn and two constables who had rushed from Daleswick to the scene as soon as they heard of the explosion. Sid Jessop spoke to the sergeant and the three policemen escorted Sid, Bert and Tilsley to the works superintendent's office, where Mr Beaulieu awaited a report of the day's events.

'What happened, Jessop?' enquired Beaulieu once the three colliers had entered his office and closed the door.

'We have reason to believe the explosion was caused by a discarded cigarette, sir,' answered the foreman.

'Good God,' declared Beaulieu. 'What bloody fool did it?' he added.

Jessop stared at Tilsley, hardly containing his contempt and disgust. 'We have reason to believe it was Tilsley sir, who's been nothing but trouble ever since he started.'

He pointed a long, accusing finger directly at Tilsley so there was no doubt that his boss knew who the culprit was.

Jessop continued: 'The foreman at Daleswick warned me about him, sir, but I still took him on. I thought he was just a boy, and everyone deserves a second chance.'

The Hillthorpe pit foreman glared at Tilsley with contempt, bordering on hatred.

'Six weeks ago Jethro Toon told me that he had caught Tilsley smoking and I thought the boy had learned his lesson. And now this. . .' his voice stuttered with repressed emotion, a combination of fury with the perpetrator and sadness for those lost and injured, before continuing: 'If you ask me he should be charged with murder – cuz that's what it is, sir.'

Beaulieu turned his attention to Tilsley.

'Well boy, what have you to say for yourself?'

'All I did, sir, was rescue that poor lad, Tommy Wagstaff. You saw me pull him out, Mr Jessop. Besides, it wasn't my cigarette sir, it was his. . .'

Tilsley pointed at Bert.

'But, but sir. . . croaked Bert, absolutely taken aback by what Tilsley had accused him of.

This downright lie was too much for the already enraged Sid Jessop, who leapt to Bert's defence before even Bert had chance to speak for himself.

'It's not this one, sir. He's a good young miner. I know him and he doesn't even smoke. Tilsley smokes like a trooper. It was him alright.'

'Sergeant Milburn, you'd better take these two to the police station in Gigthorpe for their own protection, while we investigate further.'

'Yes sir,' acknowledged the sergeant.

He and his two constables escorted Bert and Tilsley out of the door. Once outside the superintendent's office pandemonium broke loose. Word had got around that Tilsley had caused an explosion with his stupidity and a baying crowd, especially the relatives of the dead men and little Joe Sydon, wanted vengeance.

The three policemen had great difficulty getting the two teenagers to their van and had to rely on Sid Jessop and some of the other senior colliers to hold back the angry crowd. It took five men alone to hold back Jethro Toon from fulfilling his promise to Archie Tilsley.

Six weeks later, after a full board of inquiry – instigated by the mine owners, union representatives, local magistrates and the police – it came to the conclusion that no case could be proven.

Tilsley insisted it was Bert Dyson who threw the cigarette into Dame Nellie; Bert Dyson alleged it was Archie Tilsley who was guilty. Despite every member of the inquiry board believing without hesitation that Tilsley was the guilty party, they all knew that, without any witnesses, in a court of law there could be no prosecution as there could be claimed 'reasonable doubt'. It came simply to Tilsley's word against Dyson's.

The miners were incensed and vowed to toughen up safety procedures even more. The management were sorry that no culprit was found but were anxious to get production back as soon as possible. They offered three months wages to each of the dead miners' families as compensation – the unions, they reasoned to themselves, would provide after that.

Bert returned to the Hillthorpe pit soon after and he was greeted with warmth and friendship by all the colliers young and old – especially by a grateful Tommy.

Archie Tilsley never returned to his home village of Daleswick. He just went missing.

# Chapter Six

*November 1915:*

One winter Saturday afternoon in 1915, the lads had finished their shift which had started at 5am. They were watching a local football match between their village Hillthorpe and a pit side from the next colliery, Daleswick. Being from Daleswick, Bert supported his team and he reminded Tommy of their 'obvious superior skills' compared to the 'clod hoppers' of Hillthorpe. His friend replied that if they were so good how come Bert wasn't playing for them? Bert, for once, couldn't find the answer to that.

It was a bright, beautiful day, with a slight chill in the air and one, unknown to the two young colliers, that would change their lives forever.

Hundreds of men and boys, many of whom were uplifted by a few lunchtime ales, roared their approval and disappointments at the twenty-two figures and three officials in the battle being carried out on a slag heap of a pitch.

'It's not St James's Park,' quipped Bert, as he surveyed the quagmire of the churned up playing surface before him.

'Nay Bert, no poor sod ought to be playing on that,' replied Tommy.

At half-time the colliery band played catchy and patriotic

songs and local lasses crowded around the handsome line of soldiers, who marched in step to the music in front of the pavilion. The platoon of the King's Own North Yorkshire Volunteers looked mighty impressive, kitted out with their smart, khaki tunics, shiny buttons, gleaming boots and regulation caps. The orderly and well presented soldiers made a sharp contrast to the mob of scruffy miners, many of whom were still black from their labour and in their eagerness to watch 'the match' had not bothered to go home and clean up.

'Come on, son,' barked the recruiting sergeant to Tommy, whose height made him stand out in the crowd. 'We could do with a few big men like you. Are you going to serve your King and Country and protect the lady folk?'

As the expectant eyes of the crowd of people swarming around the army display looked at Tommy, he remembered what his Ma had told him when the war first started in the summer of the previous year.

'You join up son, and I'll never see you again. Don't let them take my Tommy away, promise me Tom, promise me,' she implored with beseeching eyes.

Ma wasn't the sort of woman to indulge in emotion; she couldn't afford to with a family to feed, wash and clothe and a husband, whose lungs, wrecked by coal dust, meant that his health would never be the same again – nor give him the pride of putting 'bread on the table'.

Tommy could see his Ma's pleading eyes willing him to go home that very moment, pulling him with an invisible, loving cord. Everybody was looking at him and he wasn't used to being the centre of attention. Part of him wanted to run, to go back to the little two bedroomed terrace house he called home – where he knew his Ma and Da and his two brothers and sister would be, where they would always be.

Tommy was confused. All those people staring at him; the recruiting sergeant with his enormous arm clamped around him in a cheery, matey embrace; the girls from the nearby sorting shed

38

urging him coyly to 'make his mark'. He felt giddy with it all –
the rhythmic pom-pom of the martial music, the glow of pride
when the friendly sergeant picked him out from all the boys at the
pit, all on top of the slightly intoxicating brew and fresh bravado
he felt from his third pint. It was nice of the sergeant to buy him
that drink he thought, he didn't even know him.

But again he thought of Ma and again he faltered. He couldn't
let her down. For months all the men and boys had been talking
about 'joinin' up' to do their bit, and most found any possibility
of getting away from the pit an attraction.

Although miners were nationally exempt from 'the call to
arms', being an essential industry to feed the nation's 'war
machine', it did not stop thousands of young men joining up to
get away from the harshness of their everyday existence.

'No,' thought Tommy. 'What about Ma, what about the rest of
the family who depend on my wages?'

He was a seam worker now and, though just seventeen,
Tommy was already earning top money at the pit where his youth
and strength ensured that he could dig out coal as fast as men five
years older than him.

'Victor and Edward would soon be of age though,' he thought.
'Soon they'll be bringing in the same money and they'll look
after Ma and Da and little Emma.'

Then he recalled what Ma implored him, only a few days
before, when she said: 'You're too young, son. Please don't join
up Tommy, don't leave me.'

His thoughts were interrupted by the booming voice of the
recruiting sergeant.

'Come on, son, just make your mark. Make your Mam proud
of you. The Army will make a real man of you.'

But Tommy dithered, unsure and torn between wanting to
impress the sergeant, the girls from the sorting shed and his mates
or having to face his beloved Ma, knowing how much it would
hurt her.

Again he hesitated and was about to turn away when his mate

Bert grasped the initiative. It was Bert who had always led Tommy – but not in a domineering way; it was just that Bert had done this ever since they began at the colliery. Bert had that extra spark and somehow Tommy was always happy to go along with whatever his pal did – within reason. His friend always seemed to Tommy to have a sense of fun and adventure, but any mischief he got himself into never held any malice. Besides, Bert had saved his life and Tommy, being physically larger than his popular pal, felt a little protective towards him.

Bert stepped up to the sergeant and gave a big, comic salute, ready to 'give his mark'. He basked in the moment and the girls cheered and the pit boys howled their approval.

'I've always wanted a decent pair of boots,' joked Bert. 'And you promise there won't be any coal dust in my beer, Sarge?'

The sergeant slapped Bert on the back, he had a new 'hero' now, and the soldier laughed out aloud as the crowd joined in the bonhomie.

'Somebody's got to keep Bert out of trouble,' figured Tommy.

Instinctively Tommy lined up behind his pal Bert. Bert didn't say anything, he didn't have to, and Tommy just thought it was the right thing to do.

'Where do I sign?' piped up Bert, as he clearly savoured his moment of glory. He gave his details and scratched his name on the paper on top of the wooden barrel of beer used as a bureau for the occasion. Tommy did the same.

'That's it lads,' beamed the sergeant. 'You're King's men now, go and line up with the rest of the men.'

Bert and Tommy fell in with the other raw recruits, and Bert flailed his arms, stiffened his back and stood to attention – much to the amusement of the sergeant and the crowd.

'No more mines for you lot, no more digging. You're one of us now: The King's Own North Yorkshire Volunteers,' bellowed the sergeant. 'Attention, right turn. Quick march.'

Tommy and Bert followed with the fifty-two other new recruits from the surrounding North Riding villages. They marched behind the smart soldiers in time to the pom-pom-pom of the bass drum. Tommy's chest swelled with pride as he passed the cheering crowd who came to see a football match and were now congratulating the boys and men who had enlisted that afternoon.

A few minutes later the well wishers were behind them as the recruits and the soldiers trooped half a mile to the coal railway station, where a train awaited to whisk them off to the nearest boot camp sixty miles away. Soon the delirium Tommy felt when he first signed his name evaporated as the effects of the alcohol wore off and he wondered what his Ma had made for his tea that evening. A private shouted at him to get into the railway carriage, and 'move his backside'.

That day was the last time Tommy saw his Ma.

# Chapter Seven

*December 1915:*

Moorsby Camp, in the desolate wild moors of the North Yorkshire Riding in December 1915, was not the most enticing of places to be, but to a bunch of mostly teenage recruits, many of whom had never even wandered five miles from their homes before, it was 'the pits'. Even those who used to work in the pits agreed with that.

The constant drizzle of sleet and the biting cold brought by the cutting north easterly winds only added to their general misery. Not to forget. . . of course. . . their new 'best friend' as he liked to call himself – Corporal Tilsley.

Tommy and Bert could not believe it when they marched into camp, lined up on 'the square', and were greeted by the NCOs. There, standing before them, was Archie Tilsley, with two stripes on his uniform. On recognising the two new recruits instantly, his features burst into a wide, malevolent grin at his piece of 'luck'.

'Well, well, well, look who it is,' he beamed. 'If it isn't that little runt Dyson and his faithful lap dog. 'Aven't got a ciggie, 'ave you, Dyson? I know you must be gaspin' for one,' he snarled, before bursting out in laughter at his own 'joke'.

Bert and Tommy stood there to attention, each feeling a hatred for a man who was still equally despised in Hillthorpe and Daleswick.

'Eyes front, shoulder arms,' yelled the NCO.

Forty-two men instinctively turned their heads and lifted their ancient and cumbersome Lee Enfields onto their shoulders – although not in perfect unison.

'Bloody useless bunch of Tykes,' bawled Corporal Tilsley. 'A bag of ferrets have got better co-ordination than you miserable lot of nancy boys.'

'Ra-aise arms!' he squawked.

The men lifted their heavy guns above their heads.

Tilsley continued: 'On the spot running. . . Go!'

The platoon responded to the command but after less than a couple of minutes many of the young troopers began to flag with the effort. Tilsley strutted along the faltering line until he 'found' Sapper Dyson – standing directly in front of him before moving in closer so their noses almost touched.

'Pick your pace up Dyson, you slovenly excuse for a soldier.'

Bert responded by stepping faster, but his efforts were at a cost. When his legs pumped harder his arms visibly weakened and he dropped his rifle – much to the delight of the corporal.

'Decided to quit, 'av you, lad. Well, obviously you need some more practice.'

Tilsley smiled to himself, an action which did not go unnoticed by Tommy, who was running on the spot next to Bert.

'Platoon, shun!' screamed Tilsley, his command almost inaudible but the grateful troops picked up its meaning in an instant. The men were much relieved to stop and many panted heavily after their exertion.

'Platoon, dismissed,' barked the corporal, which was music to the ears of the knackered squaddies.

Tommy picked up Bert's rifle and handed it to his exhausted friend.

'Not you Dyson. You need more training. Now raise arms and run around the square. Jump to it you lazy lump of shite!'

Bert looked at Tommy in despair but there was no getting away from it. Further protests would be futile and just attract more punishment.

Tommy faced the corporal. 'But Corporal. . .' he said, but Tilsley did not let him continue.

'You want to join him Wagstaff?' interrupted Tilsley, said as if it was a challenge.

Tommy, incensed by the pointless punishment to his friend, stared at the NCO with contempt and then, much to Tilsley's surprise, raised his rifle above his head and trotted behind Bert. Bert glanced at Tommy and offered a weak smile, giving a nod in gratitude of this unsolicited support by his mate.

Tilsley scoffed to himself and let the two sappers endure the rigours of his parade ground exercise until he had the enjoyment of seeing Bert fall down in complete exhaustion – only then did the corporal make his exit to the nearby NCO hut for a 'deserved' cup of tea and a bacon sandwich for his morning's work.

For the next fifteen weeks the gruelling training continued. Six o'clock reveille, kit and hut inspections, drill on the parade ground and endless marching over the surrounding moors.

After a few months the men considered themselves 'veterans' of the army boot camp, and openly jeered and 'took the mickey' when the next unfortunate cadre of raw recruits marched disjointedly through the gates of Moorsby Camp.

Despite the improvement in the platoon's parade ground co-ordination, their fitness levels, team-work, and general appearance more befitting regular soldiers, there was one important factor that all the trainees unanimously agreed never took a turn for the better – their food.

Tommy, Bert, and most of the platoon could not believe that they were expected to meet the physical standards demanded by the British Army on the meagre rations they were given. Many of the lads, especially those who came from the industrial cities such as Leeds or Middlesbrough, were used to a basic diet. Some were positively skeletal and showing signs of consumption –

conditions which had been turned a blind eye to by recruiting sergeants, desperate to fill their ever increasing quotas.

But, as the young soldiers reasoned to themselves in the 'luxury' of their platoon bivouacks, surely they were all in the same boat and the army knew what it was doing. It was part of the toughening up process, wasn't it? It must always be like this for new recruits!

'There is a war on!' came the conclusion of one astute squaddie.

It wouldn't be in anyone's interest to dish out inadequate rations to their fighting men – so they had to do what the British soldier had been continuing to do for centuries. Grin and bear it!

But it didn't stop them grumbling amongst themselves as their stomachs were rumbling.

'You hungry, Tommy?' Bert asked, but it was a pointless question as he already knew the answer.

'Aye, I am Bert,' answered Tommy, hoping that Bert might have a secret food stash he might be willing to share. 'How about you?'

Tommy knew Bert didn't need any encouragement to talk about his favourite subject for the past six weeks – food.

'My stomach,' responded Bert with a voice which combined self pity and humour, 'is rumbling like two pit props creaking under the strain. I swear if I don't 'ave anything to eat in the next ten minutes my innards are going to cave in.'

Tommy laughed out loud; only Bert could make a joke in such dire circumstances, but it did not hide the fact that he was right – it was not just them but the whole platoon was suffering and showing signs of near starvation.

The pair were on the daily foot slog across the moor with the rest of the cadre. It was the middle of January and the short days had already drawn in. The ground was sodden and slippery and the men struggled to keep their feet. With full pack, webbing and rifle each soldier was carrying at least 50lbs – even more if the poor unfortunate had the extra burden of a Lewis gun or its ammunition.

However, the NCOs 'on guard' called the route march 'a stroll in the park!' The men staggered along, mostly in silence as they did not have the energy after enduring nine miles without rest.

The only 'encouragement' they had was the three NCOs – one being Cpl Tilsley himself – going up and down the line shouting venomously at any 'stray' who was struggling to keep up the pace – like three snarling sheepdogs keeping their flock in order. Mind you, all the poor sappers knew that the NCOs had far more energy to shout because they weren't weighed down with heavy kitbags and they had, much to the men's chagrin, enjoyed a decent breakfast to start their day – a luxury the men could only dream of!

Senior Corporal Garthwaite did not like what he saw; the men looked exhausted after only a short trek. He didn't mind that, that was to be expected with a bunch of raw recruits, but what he did not want was any of the men collapsing under the duress. It not only meant the 'bloody shirker' would have to be carted back to camp but it would mean 'the weakling' would have to report to the MO. Besides, Cpl Garthwaite, did not want, in any circumstances, any of his cadre dying on the moor of a 'friggin' heart attack', he reminded his fellow corporals. 'Think of the paperwork,' he told them – and if there was one thing that Cpl Garthwaite feared it was paperwork – not surprising for a man who could hardly read or write.

'Platoon, halt!' he barked; no sooner had the word 'halt' come out of his mouth than the men stopped and stood to welcome attention.

'Ten minutes, kit and uniform inspection. Diss...missed.'

Forty-two men hit the floor simultaneously on the most comfortable piece of moorland they could find. Most sat with their backs against a stone wall that protected a farmer's field. Tommy lay his rifle up against the wall but the more mercurial Bert had other ideas than just a spot of recuperation.

'Time to go over the top, Tommy, me lad,' he said.

Tommy looked at Bert with a quizzical expression.

46

'Over the wall, Tom,' perhaps a little slower than normally. 'There's a farmer's field and you don't know what we might find.'

Tommy still did not know what his friend was talking about.

'Food, Tommy!' exclaimed Bert, with a hint of exasperation. 'Where there's a farmer's field, there's food,' he changed his tone to a whisper as he did not want to alert others.

The other soldiers around them were oblivious to Bert and Tommy scampering over the wall; thankfully, so were the NCOs, who sat fifty yards away, each enjoying puffing away on a Woodbine. Even though it was only around 4pm the light was fast beginning to fade, which helped make the two desperadoes little escapade easier.

Over the wall, Bert quickly appraised his target. He took his bayonet and began to scrape the soil, which was reluctant to part; it was not long before he espied his treasure. From the dark, earthy mud he pulled out a sorry little spherical object covered in sludge and of undetermined colour. Bert lifted it up to Tommy's face in triumph, wiping away the dirt with his hands before proclaiming: 'Look, Tommy mate, food,' and a great grin spread across his face.

'What is it, Bert?' Tommy asked excitedly.

'A swede,' came the reply, and with that Bert tried to eat it by gnawing at the vegetable but that proved a fruitless exercise, as the swede was rock solid, frozen to its core.

This minor setback did not deter Bert's enthusiasm and he encouraged Tommy to join him gathering as many swedes as time allowed. While they were groping about in the mud Wally Smethick stuck his head over the wall and called in a low voice so none of the NCOs could hear:

'What you doin' lads?'

'Harvesting, Wally, harvesting,' replied Bert.

'Well, bleedin' get on with it, 'cause Tilsley's finished his fag and about to head this way,' warned their friend.

'Quick Tommy, grab what you can and get back over the wall,' said Bert.

The two soldiers tried to carry as many swedes as they could muster but the little, round vegetables kept falling to the ground – each time Bert and Tommy tried to pick one up another fell down, which made Wally smile.

'Here Wally, catch,' instructed Bert, and he threw a swede, rapidly followed by three more, which his friend caught with some aplomb.

Tommy and Bert both then managed to climb back over the wall just before Cpl Tilsley came into view – though they must have looked suspicious as they were both puffing and panting and at the same time stuffing swedes into their bags and anywhere else they could find to conceal them.

'How can you two still be out of breath, you've been sitting on your backside for the last ten minutes. Remind me later to give you a spot more PE,' he smirked, pleased with his own witty remarks.

'Platoon. . . on your feet,' shouted Cpl Garthwaite and forty-two squaddies moaned and groaned in unison but all responded.

'Platoon. . . march!'

Tommy, Bert and Wally soon stepped in rhythm but their aching bodies did not appreciate this new exertion – especially now that each had about 3lbs more to carry the three miles back to Moorsby Camp.

That evening Tommy and Bert tucked into a new course on their menu. Outside their tent, after previously consuming the meagre rations of the canteen, they used a billie can to boil their captured vegetables – even Bert had given up trying to eat them raw.

The result was a coarse, tasteless inedible pulp, which despite being exposed to heat for a good 30 minutes, still refused to completely cook and proved even harder to digest. While Wally and Tommy gave up after attempting a few mouthfuls, Bert doggedly persevered – somehow managing to consume two of the swedes in their entirety.

49

That night was not the best of Bert's life as the effects of his feast soon began to haunt him – it also disturbed Tommy who was sharing his billet.

After 'throwing up' three times Bert now needed to empty his bowels – quick! He rushed out at least three times that night in the freezing rain. When he did manage to get back to his blankets and lay there he soon returned to holding his stomach, doubled up and sweating

'You all right, Bert?' enquired a concerned Tommy. He coaxed him with a water bottle to make sure his pal had some more fluids.

'I'll be all right, Tom,' Bert replied in a weak voice. 'I'll just sleep it off. The stomach cramps are the worst.'

At that moment another 'urge' came across Bert and he rushed out of the tent in the direction of the latrine – a path that he was now well familiar with.

The next morning Tommy woke to find Bert already up but as white as a sheet, having obviously not slept and suffered in the night.

'How do you feel now Bert?' asked Tommy.

'Lousy, Tommy. I'll never eat another swede again. I swear. I had more runs last night than Jack Hobbs in a test match at Lords.'

Tommy didn't know much cricket, he was a football man, but even he had heard of the Surrey and England batting maestro. Tommy couldn't help but laugh. How could Bert, he thought, find something humorous to say in the state he was in; Tommy could only admire him.

That second Wally Smethick appeared at the flap of the tent with a pair of swedes in his hands.

'More swedes any one!' he said with a big toothy grin and looking at Bert.

'You bast. . .' Bert only managed to splutter out before once again he held his stomach and ran out the exit in double quick time, heading for the sanctuary of the latrines.

# Chapter Eight

*February 1916:*

One February evening Tommy and Bert were passing the NCOs'
hut and happened to glance in the frosted window. There before
them Quartermaster Savage, Cpl Bulger and Cpl Tilsley were
tucking into their evening meal.

Tommy enviously eyed the meat, potatoes and vegetables
which he observed on the plates before the NCOs, who were too
busy engaged in their food and conversation to notice the two
soldiers staring through the glass. A white coated attendant
brought a steaming hot boat of gravy and Tilsley beckoned the
man to pour some on to his already overloaded plate. Another
attendant was seen carrying out the empty soup dishes – a course
already consumed by the three diners.

Bert looked at Tommy in amazement. They hadn't seen such a
feast since they enlisted and neither had the rest of their platoon.

'Come on, Tommy, I'm sure there's a hard tack biscuit in my
kitbag back at the hut,' joked Bert. 'Would sir care to join me?'

Tommy smiled and politely added: 'I'll bring the wine, good
sir,' and patted his water bottle, which was strapped around his
neck and hung by his hip.

The winter of early 1916 was not kind to the occupants of

Moorsby Camp and the icy temperatures and biting winds only added to their misery. The British Army does not stop its training for 'a spot of inclement weather' – especially when its appetite for troops to replace the dead and maimed on the fields of Flanders and Northern France needed urgent replenishment.

Often Tommy and Bert found themselves on the unpopular 'ghost' shift when it came to camp guard duty – courtesy of Cpl Tilsley who organised the rotas. One early morning they were at the wooden sentry boxes either side of the main entrance, and although these part shelters gave some respite from the rain or sleet they did nothing to insulate the occupants from the cold. Flapping and bracing their arms against themselves to keep warm, or stamping their feet, was the only way for Tommy and Bert to fight off the biting chill; the inadequate army issued tunics barely fit for purpose to shut out the cold, as the sodden moisture in the North Yorkshire air made every movement of their limbs heavier and heavier.

It was 4.54am and still two hours to go before their guard duties came to an end. The darkness covered the moorlands like a black blanket and there were no signs of activity from the many starlings, thrushes, kites and other local bird life yet to be wakened from their slumbers.

'You hungry, Bert?' asked a bored Tommy, ''cuz I am.'

'Still two hours and six minutes to breakfast, Tom,' replied Bert, 'but whose countin'? Can't wait for that knob of bread and that drippin'. That drippin' tastes like kerosene, but I'm so glad to eat somethin' that I must admit it gets more tasty every day. My stomach kept it down for the first time yesterday,' he joked, not without some exaggeration, and the pair chuckled.

As they stood gazing out into the black void, just making out the first twenty yards of road leading from the camp, they both felt the futility of their situation and the monotony of their thankless task.

Bert tried to change the subject away from food, a tactic to avert the emptiness in both their stomachs.

'Look Tom, why don't you write to your mam? Yer, 'aven't written her since we marched off. She's bound to be worried about you. Just let her know yer all right, lad.'

The simple request tore right through Tommy and a powerful surge of guilt and shame rose from within him. The feelings were compounded by the fact that it was a fair question from his best mate, concerned for him, his mam and the rest of his family.

'I can't, Bert, I can't,' he blurted, not helped by a sudden choke in his throat. 'I let her down badly. She won't forgive me. I promised not to leave her and the family. . . and I did.'

'But Tommy, she'll forgive you. She's your Ma; Mas forgive their bairns anything. She knows. We're at war, you joined up to save our country – to defend her, Emma, your Da, your brothers and everythin' you hold dear.

'Tommy, lad, 'er feelin's for you won't change because you gave in on the spur of the moment. I was the one who got you into joining up. If anyone's to blame, blame me. Just write to her, let her know yer thinkin' of her; it would mean so much to her. Please Tom,' said Bert with compassion in his voice.

'I can't, I just can't. I can't look her in the eyes – I betrayed her; she doesn't deserve it. The family depended on me, especially with Da in such bad 'ealth,' replied Tommy, becoming more agitated with every word spoken.

'But Tom. . . your Ma, she. . . ' Bert tried to interrupt.

'I don't want to talk about it. It's none of your business. Don't say another word on the subject or I'll, I'll... '

There was a pause as Tommy's emotions threatened to spill out, although he couldn't find the next words to express himself.

Bert realised he had hit a nerve and, noting Tommy's building anger and frustration, decided not to pursue the subject any further at the danger of causing a rift between him and his best pal.

Fortunately for Bert, at that exact moment a stray sheep came into his view, nibbling at a piece of tough, moorland grass by the camp's perimeter fencing.

Bert lifted his rifle and in a raised and authoritative voice, demanded of the 'intruder': 'Who goes there? Come forward and identify,' following the challenge as laid down in the King's Army manual.

The sheep duly responded by turning its head, giving Bert a pensive glare, and emitting a long 'Baaaa' before returning to its moorland breakfast.

'Sorry, Captain Morrison. Didn't recognise you, sir,' quipped Bert.

Tommy, a second before deep in despondency, was snapped out of his doldrums by this momentary encounter.

'At least he knew tonight's watchword, Bert,' said the now grinning Tommy, and the pals both laughed. Another five minutes had passed to breakfast time.

At seven o'clock precisely the two tired trainee troopers were greatly relieved when they finally reported to the gate's duty NCO, Corporal Atkins, at the Sergeant's office. They were replaced by two other squaddies – both, noted Tommy, with the same long faces he and Bert had possessed four hours earlier in anticipation of their impending sentry duty.

Just as they were about to turn for the canteen and their much awaited 'scram', Tommy's eye caught the front gate where two civilian trucks were rolling onto the parade ground after one of the new guards had lifted the wooden barrier at the entrance.

The letters 'C. Whittingham and Son – purveyors of fine meats, fish, fruit and vegetables' were emblazoned on the canvas sides of the Bedford vans.

As soon as they parked, the drivers alighted and were immediately met by Quartermaster Sergeant Major Savage and Cpl Tilsley. They were joined by the head 'chef' Cpl Bulger – if chef was the right description – who had all come out in haste from the canteen kitchen door, followed by six of 'his' catering staff.

Savage and Tilsley shook the hand of the elder civilian rigorously – who, Tommy quickly assumed, must be Mr

Whittingham senior – and the gesture was heartily returned as if all were good friends of long standing.

While the six canteen staff started to unload the contents of the truck under the hawk like eyes of Cpl Bulger – bags of spuds, nets of fresh vegetables, boxes of apples, tins of soups, cans of powdered milk and custard, packets of tea and a good quantity of butchered animal carcasses – the two civilians were escorted into the canteen by the three smiling NCOs as if revered guests.

Tommy and Bert began to queue up with the rest of the squaddies for their breakfast rations and as they stood waiting they saw the quartermaster and corporal, together with the civvies, being instantly given a plate of eggs and bacon, along with a pot of steaming hot tea – a rare luxury even for the camp's officers. All, again, served by white coated attendants. After they exchanged words the QSM counted out some bank notes and then a few silver coins and held them out to the elder driver, whose signature was then required on a docket, proffered by Cpl Tilsley. The man obliged and then slid a key over to Savage before the party all returned to their hearty breakfast, amid more laughter and amicable chatter.

'Come on, you dozy sapper,' barked Cpl Bulger, who now appeared behind the serving counter, as Tommy dawdled in the queue. 'You're not the only one needs feedin' boy,' and with that the corporal chef dolloped with relish an unappetising portion of semolina on to the bowl of the hungry soldier.

'What's that?' Tommy innocently queried the chief chef, wondering if he would be able to scrape the congealed offering on to his spoon quick enough before it set hard to his bowl.

'What's that?' an indignant and red faced Cpl Bulger exploded at the impudence of his fine culinary creations being questioned by the lowest member of His Majesty's Armed Forces. 'It's all you're bleedin' getting, you greedy little tyke. Now sod off!'

Tommy looked at his meagre rations and looked at Cpl Bulger before deciding any further words of query would be useless, and went to join Bert at a nearby trestle.

'Who's that with Tilsley, Bert?'

'That's Cyril Whittingham, the food merchant – a couple of the lads who come from Redcar said he's a nasty bit of work. Him and his sons don't take too kindly to any honest business competition. Heard one story that he had reversed his van 'accidentally' into a new shop front of this family who had tried to set up a fruit and veg store in Saltburn. No witnesses, of course.

'The owner was an 'Old Contemptible' and had lost an arm at the Battle of Mons; he was invalided out of the army and put all his savings into the shop.

'When the back of the van went through the glass window he was sent flying, cut to pieces and shattered the shoulder of his good arm and smashed a couple ribs too. He didn't open up again after that.

'It's Councillor Whittingham now – the lads tell me he supplies all the local schools, the hospital and this army camp. 'Ee's not without some brass.'

Tommy looked up and Cpl Bulger joined the table where Mr Whittingham and Son were being entertained by Savage and Tilsley. Bulger brought over some more hot toast and an extra portion of butter and there was more laughter. After further handshakes and back slaps the civilians departed, while Savage and Tilsley finished their considerable breakfast. When they rose to leave, Tommy, who had already polished off his food and drink a few minutes after sitting down, followed the two NCOs out of the canteen at a discreet distance.

With the Whittinghams already departed in the first truck, there, left on the parade ground, was the second one – still laden with its cargo of food supplies. Tommy, now joined by Bert, watched as Tilsley and QSM Savage climbed into the cab and drove the truck out of the camp. The guards scurried in double-quick time to lift the barrier to let them out – aided by some abuse from Cpl Tilsley to speed up their response. Savage, in the driving seat, turned the wheel to the left and the vehicle headed in the direction of Maltby – the nearest town eighteen miles away.

Later that day Tommy and Bert were outside their bivouac trying, in vain, to dry out their washed leggings – which were saturated in mud from the previous day's exercises over the moors.

Suddenly there was the distinctive honk of a horn at the main gate and he heard raised voices. Tommy put down the puttees and went towards the commotion and saw that QSM Savage and Cpl Tilsley had returned in a taxi to the camp.

They were obviously in high spirits and paid off the driver, who looked to Tommy as if he was glad to see the back of them, the two NCOs each had a cigar in hand, with Savage holding what looked like a spirit bottle in his other.

'Attention,' the inebriated corporal ordered the guards, and when the two responded by snapping to attention Savage and Tilsley burst out laughing, impressed, no doubt, at the power of their command.

Their boorish drunken behaviour disrupted those soldiers who had the misfortune to cross their path that mid afternoon. There was great relief among the men when the two NCOs staggered into the refuge of the corporals' mess to continue their drinking.

Bert came up behind Tommy and said: 'Must have cost them a bundle for that taxi, the nearest one's in Maltby. Anyway, they went out in that Bedford, didn't they?

'That's right, Bert,' said Tommy, 'they did. Follow me,' and he headed straight for the corporals' mess. Tommy looked in the window, while Bert made sure nobody was looking, and observed Savage and Tilsley polishing off the bottle. The obnoxious pair were soon joined by Cpl Bulger.

'What's happening?' asked Bert, anxious for a report.

'Savage's got out a wad of money and he's sharing it out with Tilsley and Bulger.'

It did not take Tommy long before he put two and two together and came to his conclusion.

'They must have been selling our rations and keeping the profits,' he told Bert. 'They're in it with Wittingham, Bert. All the

57

boys are starving and they are taking food out of our mouths and putting the money in their pockets. That second lorry was purely their profits and they've probably been out selling its load at the market in Maltby.'

'The thieving' bastards,' exclaimed Bert, who was not one to use profanity on a regular basis; but the words were only the echo of Tommy's thoughts.

However, unbeknown to them, Tommy and Bert at that moment were not the only one to come to that same conclusion about the dodgy dealings of QSM Savage and Cpl Tilsley – and word quickly spread around camp that the crooked pair and Cpl Bulger were profiteering from the men's misery. Their coming back drunk in a taxi after leaving, for the third month in a row, with half the camp's food rations, had aroused many suspicions – especially from men who were suffering from enforced malnutrition.

Without any prompting by Tommy and Bert there was soon an angry mob of soldiers outside the corporals' mess hut. Their anger soon stirred them into action when one of the soldiers decided to hurl a brick through the hut window. This certainly caught the instant attention of Savage, Tilsley and Bulger as it landed smack on their table, knocking over the whisky bottle and scattering monies on the floor.

The three bad tempered NCOs came out to confront the culprit, not realising the storm they were about to face or that this situation was not fully under their control – which was the usual state of affairs at Moorsby Camp.

Seeing around fifty angry men before them out for their blood they did their best to muster as much authority as they could – but it soon became obvious to them it was to little effect.

'Thieving bastards,' shouted one enraged squaddie.

'Steal our food while you pig it up in there, would you?' came another young soldier, shaking his fists at the trio.

'Give 'em' a good kickin' lads,' taunted another.

Cpl Bulger went a distinct shade of white and the danger of the situation quickly sobered up Savage and Tilsley.

Savage, a bull of a man, went on the offensive and tried in vain to assert his previously unquestioned authority but was jeered and shouted down by the furious squaddies.

Tilsley, in desperation, called for the guard but the guard did not quite hear him, or more accurately, did not want to.

Just when it looked as if the situation might turn from abuse to outright violence, Lieutenant Carsley and a troop of twenty armed regulars arrived on the scene.

Carsley fired a shot into the air from his Browning pistol and immediately there was silence from the dissenters.

'Glad you're 'ere, sir,' bluffed Savage. 'Some toe rag, sir, has put a brick through the mess window and we came to see what the palaver is all about, sir.'

Unfortunately for QSM Savage this just brought about an even more irate reaction from the men, and immediately Lt Carsley was surrounded by about thirty irate trainee soldiers, including Bert, who simultaneously told the young officer why they were so incensed.

Lt Carsley knew an angry crowd when he saw one and recognised there must be good reason for the cause of such venom, which was bordering on mutiny. He also knew by reputation and experience the likes of QSM Savage and Corporals Tilsley and Bulger.

'Sergeant Couling,' called Carsley in a raised voice.

'Yes sir,' and up sprung the sergeant, rifle at the ready.

'Escort these three NCOs to Captain Morrison's office and take these two with you,' ordered the lieutenant, pointing out Tommy and Bert to the sergeant.

'Yes sir,' obeyed Sgt Couling, who wheeled away and organised his soldiers to take the party through the crowd of belligerent and hungry squaddies.


Captain Morrison was not pleased. Lt Carsley had outlined the situation to the camp commander, including the serious accusations of the men. Capt Morrison questioned Tommy and Bert, while the three NCOs were under guard outside – their answers only confirmed his suspicions.

He too knew of these NCOs' reputations and, like Carsley, he believed the men.

Capt Morrison ordered the accused before him and asked them what they had to say for themselves.

Quartermaster Savage, not without some arrogance, replied that these were false accusations, and there was 'not a grain of truth' in them.

An unfortunate turn of phrase, thought the well educated Lt Carsley.

Savage told the captain the men were always complaining of being hungry – 'that's what all soldiers do. Grumble.' Then contradicting himself, he added, 'No soldiers had ever complained to him before about the food!'

'And you, corporal, what have you got to say for yourself?' asked the captain, now fixing his attention on Tilsley.

'It's all lies, sir, it's like the QSM says. All the men are given equal rations according to the British Army manual. These men are always complaining about their hunger sir; this is a training camp, preparing men to kill in a war – it's not the Savoy Hotel.'

Captain Morrison did not like Tilsley's impertinent answer, and he visibly frowned when the corporal had finished speaking. He did not believe one word the NCOs had told him.

'Turn out your pockets, all three of you,' commanded the captain.

'But sir,' countered a squirming QSM who knew he must stall such an order and its consequences, but the interjection had fallen on deaf ears.

The three reluctantly did as they were told until there was enough cash on the table, made up of notes, guinea pieces and silver coins, to finance a week's stay at the Savoy.

Captain Morrison's face confirmed he was not amused.

'Lieutenant, go to the QSM's office and the one in the kitchen and take every docket for the past three months,' he ordered.

Lt Carsley saluted, bade, 'Yes sir,' and left the room.

The three culprits looked at each other – Bulger with fear in his eyes, the QSM with a resigned indignation but Tilsley showing signs of a deepening rage – angry at having been caught in the first place.

Captain Morrison ordered Sgt Couling and his men to escort the three to the guardhouse and keep them confined, subject to further inquiries.

As they went out of the door Tilsley turned to Bert and hissed threateningly under his breath, just enough, so Capt Morrison could not hear, 'I'll get you for this, Dyson. You wait. I'll get you, you little turd.'

After they left, Tommy and Bert were dismissed.

Thirty minutes later Lt Carsley returned with a box of documents and more files carried by an administrative private.

'Sir, we have had a quick audit and nothing adds up. The dockets from this morning show that the deliveries signed for do not match the food which is presently in the canteen storeroom. At least half of it is unaccounted for. . . and that's just today.'

'I know,' said the distraught captain, 'I should have acted earlier.'

Morrison knew that it would be his head on the block if the auditors from headquarters got a whiff of this scandal. His promotion prospects, if any, depended on how he reacted to the present situation.

He addressed Carsley but was really talking to himself.

'I've never seen so many men in the sick bay – dysentery, fainting, hacking coughs and even a couple of cases of pneumonia and TB – they all can't be malingerers. The doc's been complaining for weeks and threatened to go above my head but I persuaded him otherwise. It's those thieving NCOs, all right. If I don't deal with this now and make sure those three are punished then we will have a strike on our hands, even a mutiny. That would be disastrous!

'Right Carsley,' he decided. 'Go through those dockets with a fine-toothcomb and interrogate those three tomorrow. Concentrate on Bulger, he'll break first. I want this kept in camp and I don't want HQ sticking their nose in.'

'Yes sir, understood, sir,' replied the lieutenant with a smart salute.

'And another thing,' added Capt Morrison. 'Make sure the men get a decent meal tonight. No more complaints.'

'Yes sir.' Carsley wheeled away to do his duty.


A week later Lance Corporal Savage and Privates Tilsley and Bulger were being treated to the delights of His Majesty's prison garrison in Colchester for a lengthy spell to point out the error of their ways.

Private Bulger did not pass on his compliments to his fellow army chef in charge of the Colchester camp's cuisine that day.

# Chapter Nine

In March 1916, on completion of their basic training, the newly formed regiment of the King's Own North Yorkshire Rifles – affectionately known as the 'Norkies' prepared to leave for the battlefields of France.

After the men were fed regular rations and their young bodies responded to the weeks of physical conditioning, there was a real sense of optimism as the spring weather reflected the general air around Moorsby Camp.

The mood of the men was also improved by the fact that they no longer had NCOs such as QSM Savage and Corporal Tilsley to 'guide them'.

After his basic training, Wally Smethick was transferred to a 'Medical Corps' unit for more 'advanced training' as a stretcher bearer at an army camp in Wiltshire.

'Wherever Wiltshire is?' confided Wally to Tommy and Bert on the day he left.

The two friends felt a mixture of excitement and trepidation at the prospect of leaving for a foreign land – one beyond their imaginations only six months before – and the reality that they would be called to the front line and be using, for real, their well practised rifle skills on the Hun.

'Don't worry, Tommy,' piped up Bert, 'the politicians said it would be over by Christmas. . .' He paused before continuing, 'The only thing, lad, is that they didn't say which one!'

Tommy laughed. He was glad he had a pal like Bert; he would not have made it this far, without him, he thought.

'Look Tom,' said Bert in a more serious and considerate voice. 'We will be leaving North Yorkshire soon and we don't know what's before us. Anythin' could 'appen Tom. I ain't saying it will but there's always the chance that one of us, or even both of us, might not be coming back.'

Tommy's eyes fell to the ground in anticipation of what he knew was coming.

'Tommy, yer 'ave to see your Ma and the rest of the family. Little Emma adores you – you've broken their hearts by running away and not seeing them. This could be your last chance!'

Bert felt rotten for giving this advice but concluded that, in all conscience, he must at least try to make his pal change his mind and contact his family.

Tommy, feeling increasingly uncomfortable amid rising pangs of guilt, picked up his boots and began to buff them hard with a brush to focus his attention away from the sensitive subject.

His mind wandered to a fortnight before, when he was suddenly ordered to the guardhouse as his mother had arrived at the entrance of the camp, along with little Emma, in the hope of seeing her son. Tommy knew that the journey itself was the longest his beloved Ma and little sis had undertaken from Hillthorpe and would have cost Ma considerable expense and time, to say nothing of the discomfort to the pair of them.

'How did she find out?' he wondered.

Ma had demanded where her son was 'taken' from the works' superintendent Mr Beaulieu. She figured a man of his authority must know and one day went into his office unannounced and 'respectfully' informed him that she would not be leaving until he promised to find out. Mr Beaulieu, realising it was easier to comply as to refuse would merely invoke more visits and interruptions, agreed 'to see what he could do'.

It did not take long for Mr Beaulieu to find out through the contacts at his disposal – made easier by that implement of modern communication the telephone, which had been newly installed in his office.

The resourceful Ma also had Tommy's whereabouts revealed by Bert and Wally's Mas – even though the British Army discouraged divulging such 'highly sensitive' information or even confirming where their troops were training.

Ma and Emma arrived at Camp Moorsby, having spent a precious three days wages of the family's budget in transport costs – especially the taxi from Maltby. It was the first and only time Ma had rode in one. The visitors were escorted to the guardhouse and despite the insistence of a sympathetic Sgt Baxter that it was not possible to see her son, an equally insistent Ma led to Lieutenant Carsley being summoned.

Lt Carsley argued that if he allowed her to see Tommy it would set a precedent – the meaning of which he had to explain to Ma. If he did, he said, the place would be inundated with 'camp followers'. The officer stressed that 'there was a war on' to which Ma replied that is exactly why she demanded to see her son 'before he was lost forever' which brought an immediate flood of tears from Emma.

This had the desired effect. Lt Carsley was not a man without compassion and reasoned that he had a mother himself, and the poor woman had made such an effort. He acquiesced to her request but 'only on condition her son agreed to see them,' the junior officer added this with a smile, which he assumed would be a formality.

However, when Sapper Wagstaff was ordered to the guardhouse by the not so compassionate Cpl Tilsley to go and see his 'mummy' Tommy went into a panic and refused to obey. He was adamant that he was not moving from his tent and Lt Carsley, not wishing to become involved in domestic matters, said to Ma that 'there was nothing he could do, reluctantly, if Sapper Wagstaff did not want to see them.'

The doting mother and her distraught daughter had no choice but to leave, and it was much to Lt Carsley's credit that he arranged for a staff car to take them to the railway station at Maltby.

'I couldn't see them, Bert, I couldn't,' blurted Tommy with tears running down his cheeks as soon as they drove away.

'Don't you see. I wanted to with all my heart. After disobeying her wishes and signin' up I just couldn't face her,' he spluttered.

'But Tom. . .' Bert tried to interrupt, but the words, for once, just flowed from his friend.

'If I saw her again I couldn't carry on, Bert. I wanted to go home, but I knew if I did I could never leave them. I would go AWOL. I'm sorry, Bert, I'm sorry.'

Tommy put his head in his hands and sobbed, something that Bert had never seen before and he pitied his friend.

Bert put his hand on Tommy's shoulder and patted it, nodding to himself without another word before walking away.

# Chapter Ten

*May 1916:*

The King's Own North Yorkshire Volunteers regiment found themselves quartered at Albert in north-east France, within hearing distance of the heavy British and German guns pounding each other's lines.

On the railway journey there the British troops did not see any sign of the thousands of wounded soldiers at stations being taken back to 'Blighty' in the opposite direction. Many of the trains carrying the wounded, many of whom were in great pain or close to death, were shunted into sidings to give priority to the trains carrying fresh troops to go unimpeded to the fronts. The high command felt it would not be 'good for morale' if the two were given the chance to meet.

It was one of the many anomalies of the war that the Norkies were employed predominantly as a rifle brigade. Most of their ranks were made up of men from North Yorkshire and County Durham, whose backgrounds ranged from bank clerks, millers, shoemakers, brewers and farriers' apprentices, to a great number of agricultural labourers. The vast majority though, were former colliers who worked in the Great North Coalfields.

With all these mining skills at its disposal the best use of the regiment would obviously have been to send it to work on the extensive mining operations being conducted on the Somme front.

Already considerable 'successes' had been achieved by both sides through burrowing under the respective enemy's defences, packing them with high explosives and detonating these to cause huge craters that sucked in to the underworld men, weapons and elaborate defences.

Indeed, at the time of the Norkies' arrival, the British Army was busy preparing its biggest operation to date in underground warfare. In advance of the expected 'Big Push' it was decided to 'shake the Boche up' on July 1, with 40,000lbs of ammonal set to be detonated at Y-Sap underneath the German lines; nearby at Lochnager another super explosion of 60,000lbs was in situ.

However, the British Army, in its wisdom and confusion of war, continued to ignore these hundreds of skilled colliers at their disposal and placed the Norkies in reserve to 'plug the gaps' where they would be needed when the situation arose. In reality their future was 'settled' amid a battle between two senior officers at British Army Headquarters, at a chateau a good six miles behind the front line.

Major Duckworth, the deputy commander of mining operations, who was under General Fawcett-Smyth, wanted the Norkies for underground duties. Major Hughcliffe, the aide-de-camp to Brigadier General Perry, who was responsible for planning operations for 3 and 4 divisions advancing in B sector on the Somme front, wanted the regiment as a rifle brigade.

Major Duckworth and Major Hughcliffe heatedly argued for days at HQ about who was going to be in command of the Norkies. The issue was decided when Major Hughcliffe 'bumped' into General Macklin himself, the British field commander-in-chief.

'Hugo' Hughcliffe and 'Jumbo' Macklin, as the general was known to his officer circle, happened to be good friends, as fellow Old Etonians who were in the same house many years before.

Over a resplendent meal and an agreeable Sauvignon, the fate of the Norkies was sealed when they came to a gentlemanly agreement.

The next day Major Duckworth received a message from a dispatch rider commanding him to relinquish any claim to the Norkies as they were to be held in reserve. It was rubber stamped by General Macklin himself.

But if the Norkies had, unbeknown to them, avoided the hell of underground warfare, they were soon to experience another sort of it on the surface.

At 07.28am on July 1, 1916 the mines of Y-Sap and Lochager exploded, causing great devastation to the German entrenchments. Backed up by a ferocious, continuous barrage from hundreds of British guns, which spewed shells on the enemy positions, it was thought that it would be only a matter of British, Canadian, Indian and other Allied troops walking into the German trenches to take their possession.

Instead, alerted about the British plans by their intelligence, the Germans retreated to their deep, well fortified bunkers. When the British advanced, the Germans came out of their shelters and manned their machine guns to deadly effect, and mowed down 18,800 men by the end of the first day. It was the most disastrous day in the bloody history of the British Army.

News of the tragedy a few miles up the road soon reached the Norkies. Mercifully for them the powers that be did not call on the regiment to be immersed in the slaughter – they were ordered to stand by.

After the failure of the British forces to make a significant breakthrough it was the Norkies' job to step into the trenches vacated by the freshly fallen.

In May that year conscription was introduced in Britain and a new wave of 500,000 men were being trained to take the fight to 'the German devils'. In the meantime, it was the Norkies' duty to hold the line in case of a counter-attack by the enemy.

Even in the summer, life in the trenches was a miserable

existence – the food inedible, supplies unreliable and for officer and foot soldier alike, just a question of surviving each day as it came. There were moments of sheer terror, the drain of the sporadic heavy shelling and mortar fire, not to mention the constant fear of being hit by a sniper's bullet. That, and the sheer boredom.

Only the rats were prospering and Tommy, who was used to being face to face with the rodents from his time down the pits, could not believe their size – some bigger than a small dog; the vermin grew fat on their diet of human flesh from the wretched decaying corpses, abandoned on 'no man's land', which were in plentiful supply.

It was around dusk that Tommy and Bert were looking forward to a much needed 'cup of Rosie Lee' – it was a wonder to them some of the phrases they had learned since joining up. The water was not of the best quality but complaints were futile.

'What you goin' to do after this is all finished, Bert?' asked Tommy, who was unusually talkative after four hours of look-out duty.

'Don't know, mate. Reckon first thing I'll do is go home and marry Bridie Grogan from the sortin' shed,' grinned Bert. 'Always fancied her. She fancies me but she just doesn't know it yet! I ain't going down the pit again though. You see. I don't think Newcastle United will 'ave me but I reckon I could walk into the Sunderland side.'

Tommy laughed.

'Sunderland. Aweh man. They wouldn't take you on Bert Dyson, you're not good enough. They would take Albert Duxall though,' joked Tommy.

'Albert Duxall, wasn't 'e that bloke in C company who got his leg shot off last week?' asked Bert.

'Exactly,' grinned Tommy and they both laughed – not at the unfortunate Albert but more at Bert's football prowess. Gallows humour was another way to help them bear their lot.

They were laughing when their noses began to detect a faint, but alien, smell; more puffs of smoke began to drift over the trench top and both men started to gasp for air.

'Gas, gas, gas!' shouted a voice to their left and soon there was pandemonium in the British front line trench.

Tommy and Bert both frantically scrambled to put on their gas masks. Immediately Tommy felt paralysed by fear; his vision was now impaired, he could hardly see Bert, who was crouching to his right; his eyes watered, mixing with the sweat dripping off his forehead. Tommy tried to breathe but the lack of air only served to force him to inhale deeper, which quickly consumed any oxygen left. Bert, who had reacted slightly quicker to the situation, sensed his friend's fear and tugged Tommy's sleeve. Tommy span around in a daze and Bert, looking at him through the mask, gave a thumbs up and the former began to calm down and regulate his breathing.

After the vicious clouds of deadly, yellow phosphorous gas finally cleared from the trenches a new threat emerged to confront the Norkies.

A wave of German infantry followed up the initial gas attack and were closing in numbers on the British trench. The British troops, still impeded by their cumbersome gas masks and afraid to take them off in fear of inhaling the lingering toxic fumes, took position to fend off the foe and began to fire.

The Germans either hit the floor or knelt to send a volley of fire into the trenches before continuing their advance once more. Some of them managed to cut through the reels of barbed wire thirty yards away protecting the British parapets, allowing their comrades to take up the charge.

Tommy and Bert cocked their rifles, ready to fire. A Lewis gun to the left opened up and after each 'rat-a-tat-tat' a score of Germans fell to the ground. Despite their losses the men of the Westphalia Brigade kept on coming until they were almost in the British front trenches.

Tommy and Bert tore off their gas masks and welcomed the new rush of air into their lungs, even though it was still foetid.

72

Bert had reasoned that if it was safe enough for the Hun to have no gas masks it must now be all right for him, too. Tommy instinctively followed his friend.

Bert took aim at the nearest advancing figure and fired; felling his target instantly, before instinctively rebolting his Lee Enfield and repeating the action with the same success.

The German soldiers were now just yards from their objective and Tommy recoiled as a green-grey figure with a picklehaube helmet charged towards him with bayonet thrust. Tommy pulled the trigger of his .303 but to his horror all he could hear was a useless click. He froze in fear as the German was now upon him and about to deliver the fatal thrust with his bayonet into Tommy's chest. Tommy tried to scream but nothing came out; at that moment an image flashed before him of his Ma in their kitchen smiling at him, wearing her apron while preparing his food – one that he had witnessed a thousand times before.

As the image evaporated and Tommy was jolted back to the moment he regained his consciousness and stared into the manic face of his attacker. He swallowed hard and prepared 'to meet his Maker'. A glint of steel flashed across his eyes from his right and a bayonet was thrust in the ribs of the German infantryman, who was leaping from a great height down towards Tommy. Tommy then saw Bert, in one moment, push the enemy soldier with all his force into the trench away from Tommy and, holding onto his rifle, make sure the bayonet held firm. The Westphalian toppled down, reeling away to Tommy's side into the bottom of the trench, and in his momentum Bert knocked his friend out of the way before he fell on top of the dead assailant.

Both Bert and the German sprawled on the trench floor in front of a shocked Tommy, locked in a deadly embrace, his friend panting hard with relief, the German exhaling his last breaths before death took its claim.

Around them more shots flew out and individual battles raged, with men grabbing anything at hand to combat their nearest opponent. One German was almost decapitated when Sapper

d

Baldwin, who had his rifle knocked out of his grasp by his assailant, grabbed a shovel propped up against the trench wall and with both hands plunged the side of its metal edge into his attacker's neck.

Just then, with the German attack having reached its zenith and their reinforcements cut down by British mortars, a whistle blew and Sgt Howie and a fresh platoon of Norkies came to the rescue of their beleaguered colleagues.

What was left of the German attacking force retreated rapidly and in disorder towards their own lines while others held their hands up in surrender.

Tommy slowly regained his senses and stared across at his friend. He nodded at Bert, words not needed to express his gratitude.

Bert just turned and stared disbelievingly at the German he had just killed. He tenderly took off the dead soldier's helmet and saw the face of a young man, no more than eighteen years old, staring into oblivion.

Bert, with a strange, ghostly expression whispered in a sadden tone: 'I killed a man. I've sinned, Tommy. I've killed flesh and blood.'

Tommy sank to the ground, relieved to be alive.

He carefully put his hand into his top pocket and pulled out the little carved figurine of the angel, blew on it and wiped it with his tunic sleeve before saying a silent prayer to St Barbara.

He thanked God he was alive, prayed for Bert, for the soul of the dead German his friend had killed and for all men that day who had the misfortune to fight for a few yards of a muddy French field.

Just a few feet away Bert, completely drained once the adrenaline of the battle had left him, violently vomited down the side of the trench wall.

# Chapter Eleven

If Tommy and Bert had not suffered enough on that dreadful July day, unbeknown to them fate was about to deliver another cruel blow.

One morning in the trenches the friends were in shocked disbelief as none other than Corporal Tilsley began to call out the names of the platoon at roll-call. When he read the name 'Dyson' he paused and with great relish, when Bert cried out the mandatory 'here Corporal', Tilsley walked over to him deliberately to reacquaint himself with his nemesis.

'Well, what a pleasure it is, Sapper Dyson, to meet you again, and you Sapper Wagstaff. I often thought of you two in the last few months during our brief separation, so you cannot possibly know how much I have been looking forward to this moment. I'm sure we can make up for lost time, can't we lads?'

With that he threw back his head and let out a deep, throaty laugh that only served to put a shiver down the spines of Bert and Tommy.

The pair later learned that the British Army had, in its wisdom, after the decimation of its forces on July 1, scoured its prisons to replace its lost manpower. Some of the 'beneficiaries' were Messrs Savage, Tilsley and Bulger.

Even this unexpected offer of 'freedom' did not come as a welcome invitation to the fiery Tilsley. The last thing he wanted was to end up in the hellfire of the Somme – why, Tilsley had not joined the army to be shot at! Being an NCO was the perfect job for him, less work than a collier, and a chance to take advantage of those who could not fight back!

No, Tilsley did everything he could to try and take a more 'reserved role' but his Colchester jailers were not persuaded and he found himself, with fifty other 'renegades' escorted, under armed guard, to the front line. Unbelievably, after another administration 'cock-up' by stressed officers and a shortage of NCOs, Tilsley was quickly reinstated to a two striper.

Soon Tilsley had the opportunity to bring the two soldiers, who he blamed for his ignominious departure from Camp Moorsby, back under his control.

A Norkies' platoon, including Sappers Wagstaff and Dyson, found themselves working to fortify the regiment's defences.

'Put your miserable backs into it,' barked the corporal. 'You think Fritz is going to wait for you to finish this lot before he's going to attack? Move it Wagstaff.'

Sapper Tommy Wagstaff of the King's Own North Yorkshire Volunteers muttered a curse – soft enough so that Corporal Tilsley couldn't hear but loud enough so that he could hear the words himself. Tommy wasn't a man to swear, his Sunday school upbringing taught him that, but even he had his limits. He cursed the soil he was digging, he cursed the wretched Hun for making him dig this stupid, bloody trench but most of all he cursed Corporal Tilsley. He didn't know who he wanted to bash most – Flippin' Fritz or that cocky little corporal, who just seemed to enjoy making the lives of the men under his command a misery for no reason but sheer spite.

The ground was hard and stony and his pathetic army issue shovel was just like every other piece of His Majesty's kit – completely useless for the very task it was designed for.

In the distance the rat-a-tat-tat of machine-gun fire pierced the

76

air; Whiz-Bangs flew overhead towards the rear to discharge their deadly shrapnel onto their targets of the British guns and the crews that manned them. All around Tommy the ground itself seemed to groan, no doubt in futile defiance of man's latest desecration of Mother Earth and his fellow creatures.

Sweat poured down Tommy's frozen body. The combination of hard, physical labour and the fear of the enemy only served to hasten his digging. In that moment it was his only escape – to lose himself with his shovel and forget the nightmare of the world all around him.

'Eh Tommy, perhaps we can dig ourselves back into the bar of the Collier's Arms,' joked Bert. 'I tell yer what, last one at the bar buys a pint, lad!'

'Aye Bert, and I'll buy the whole German army a schnapps if they take Corporal Tilsley with them,' gasped Tommy as his boot hit the shovel.

Bert laughed and winked at his pal. Tommy smiled and chuckled to himself.

# Chapter Twelve

The next day, in their trench just behind the British front lines, Tommy and Bert were 'stood down' and 'enjoying' time free from the gaze of Corporal Tilsley and the other NCOs.

The King's Own North Yorkshire Volunteers were in support of a company from the Lancashire Rifles, who were preparing for another 'Grand Assault' on the German trenches.

It was a joke amongst the Norkies that the men of the Lancashire Rifles didn't know if they were better off facing the Hun or to have a load of Yorkshiremen behind them with guns in their hands! Equally It was a joke with the Lancashire lads that they didn't know who was the real enemy – Fritz or those 'White Rose shites'. At least Fritz had an idea on how to play a decent game of football at Christmas!

It was Bert's turn to make a welcome cup of tea. Tommy was trying, without success, to dry out his puttees – at least the barbed wire has some practical use apart from keeping the Hun out, he thought. Apart from the odd mortar shell or the distinctive distant crack of rifle shot from both sides of the line, there was a relative tranquillity as the troops tried their best to enjoy the 'calm'.

Bert called out, 'Brew up, Tommy.' Tommy wiped out the

inside of his tin mug with his fingers and held it out to Bert in anticipation.

'Yer got one for me, Bertie boy,' said one of two soldiers coming up the trench.

'Aweh man, Wally Smethick, what you do'in 'ere?' said Bert with a grin on his face.

Tommy turned around, smiled in recognition, and immediately stuck out his hand to greet a welcome friend.

'You know me lads, won't turn a free cuppa down,' said Wally.

He was accompanied by Lance Corporal Percy Slaithwaite, a fellow stretcher bearer. Bert and Tommy shook hands with Percy before Bert handed over to him his full mug of hot tea.

'Don't worry, it only takes another 20 minutes to brew up another two cups of water, Walter!' half joked Bert.

Wally smiled.

'Talking of tea, lads,' said Wally. 'I heard that the Devons refused to go over the top for a second time in a day. That wuz until an officer told them that it was a trench the Boche had just captured from an Indian regiment and there was 30lbs of tea stored in its bunkers. The Devons couldn't get over quick enuff!'

The three laughed – no doubt Wally, thought Bert, had just made that up, but it was a good tale.

Wally's hands shook as he accepted the hot cup of tea offered by Tommy.

Both Bert and Tommy looked at each other; they were glad to see their old collier pal but were surprised by Wally's state. Apart from 'the shakes' he looked tired and haggard, even though he could still manage a smile and a joke. No doubt Wally thought the same of their appearance – neither had their 'Sunday best' on.

' 'Ere Wally, I reckon you and Percy got a worse job than us, looking after the wounded. It can't be easy getting them on a stretcher with all that barbed wire, craters and Fritz firing at you at the same time,' observed Bert.

Wally stared into the dregs of his tea, as if he was trying to read his own fortune. Bert and Tommy saw a deep sadness on his face, a look that they hadn't seen before on their amiable friend.

'No disrespect lads, you know that, but I'd rather be trying to pick them up and save their lives than kill another human being – even if it was Kaiser Wilhelm himself,' said Wally.

Bert sharply looked away, trying to conceal his still raw feelings after his recent nightmare in the battle for the trench a few days before.

Tommy sensed his friend's concern and offered their guests some hard tack biscuits. The stretcher bearers both refused, mainly out of courtesy, thinking that their hosts may be short on rations themselves. Fortunately the lance-corporal pierced the awkward silence.

'You got a good un there, boys,' butted in Percy. 'He's as brave as they come is Wally. He's saved many a life, single handed. Even takes care of the Boche if they're wounded.'

Wally squirmed with embarrassment but appreciated the compliment from his colleague. Bert and Tommy grinned, the former giving Wally a big slap on the back.

'I wish we had a corporal like you, Percy. We don't know which side ours is on!' added Bert, and even Wally seemed to come out of his stupor.

'Stretcher bearers,' shouted an over enthusiastic young lieutenant who had only been in the trenches a week and was yet to see 'any action'.

Wally picked up his stretcher and Percy quickly handed his cup to Bert.

They stood to attention and saluted the officer before bidding Bert and Tommy farewell. The officer commanded them to follow him as they were wanted further along the line, where the Lancashire Rifles were set to undertake a night sortie to take out a machine-gun placement.

As he passed, Wally said: 'See you lads. I don't want to see you as a customer!' half jokingly, although he also meant it sincerely.

'No problem there, Wally, I'd rather walk, thanks, than have you carry me. I seen you play in goal. You'd only drop me!' joked Bert, as the stretcher bearers ran after the officer.

# Chapter Thirteen

That night the Lancashire Rifles 'went over the top', with orders to secure the German trench 250 yards away to their front and 'take out' two machine-gun placements.

With much bravery Captain Houghton-Fforbes, who had only been at the front for less than six weeks and already had two field promotions owing to deaths of previous incumbents, led his men by example. He was ably supported by Lieutenants Cadogan and Faversham.

The Lancashire Rifles lived up to their reputation as a determined and worthy adversary in battle. However, their reputation was no armour that infamous night for the heavy casualties they sustained; victims of the deadly machine-guns that scythed them down in their hundreds. July 16, 1916 was a day that would be sealed in the history of the proud Lancashire Regiment – the colour of its Red Rose forever a deeper hue from its bloody losses on a French field.

'Stretcher bearer,' came the frequent shout from the killing fields as cries of pain and anguish pierced the smoke coated air.

Wally, with stretcher ready, adjusted his helmet, checked the strap of his medical bag for the umpteenth time and climbed the wooden ladder out of the trench in pursuance of the injured and dying. Close behind followed 'his hoppo' Percy.

Moments before they had said a short prayer together to God to be with the soldiers, on both sides, whatever their fate; Wally added his own silent prayer asking for Bert and Tommy to have extra protection.

Ahead the battle raged. The British and German troops fought as deadly mortar shells rained onto the attacking force, discharging its lethal shrapnel on the many unfortunates who crossed its path; for those who survived they still had to run the gauntlet of machine-gun and rifle fire, and at the same time negotiate the barbed wire and craters before they reached the German lines.

'Stretcher bearer,' repeated the cry, this time with more desperation in the voice.

Wally and Percy reached the casualty just thirty feet from the parapet. A soldier was cradling his pal's head and at the same time trying to hold a piece of gauze over the wounded man's stomach – desperately attempting to prevent the oozing intestines from spilling into the mud. Wally looked at the caring soldier, whose face showed relief and expectation at the stretcher bearers' arrival.

Wally and Percy took one look at the 'wounded' man and they both knew instantly he was dead – mercifully killed by shock before the pain of his dreadful injuries could reach his consciousness.

'I'm sorry, lad,' said Percy with compassion, 'he's gone.' There were a few seconds of silence as the caring soldier stared at Percy in disbelief, before softly laying his friend's head on the ground.

Wally looked at the soldier's features; in one instant they changed from that of a concerned comrade to one who had hatred and vengeance in his eye and heart. The soldier picked up his gun, took his bayonet out of its scabbard, fixed it into the rifle's nozzle and resumed his advance on the enemy, this time with a fresh resolve.

That night Percy and Wally did what they could for as many wounded and dying men – attending their wounds, administering morphine or, in many cases, giving them their last words of human comfort in this world.

Dodging the bullets and shrapnel time and time again the courageous pair ignored the needs of their own safety to tend to their fellow men who were suffering.

Picking up an injured man on their stretcher and carrying him back to their own lines and onto the Regimental Aid Post was not only dangerous but exhausting.

No muscle bound, baritone of a drill sergeant or even Field Marshal Kitchener himself could instil the sort of commitment to their duty that both Walter Smethick and Percy Slaithwaite demonstrated with exemplary undertaking. No, these two men were driven by a force more powerful than anything man could muster – they shared the same faith and truly believed that what they were doing was exactly what their Lord and Saviour would do if he was in their army boots. They were on a mission.

It was not long before they found their next 'customer' – a private in his early thirties, who although in considerable pain insisted the medics go on to the next casualty who he claimed 'is bound to be worse off than me, lads.'

Percy looked at Wally and they both nodded in agreement.

'All right private, where you hurtin'? We're not going anywhere until we've patched you up.'

'I think I took one in the shoulder, corp,' he replied, panting heavily. As Percy tended to the man's wounds, Wally passed him strips of gauze and cleansing spirits. The smell of cordite, the cries of men, the moans of the wounded, the familiar rat-a-tat of the German Mauser machine-guns and the continued crack of rifle shot pervaded the air all around. Percy examined the wound.

'You are a lucky Rifleman. A bullet has gone right through your shoulder and out the other side. Same with a leg wound. Looks like a Blighty. Now we will clean it up, patch it with a gauze and give you a dressing. Then you can get in our taxi and we'll drop you off at the RAP.'

'Tips appreciated,' added Wally, with a kindly smile.

The man attempted to smile even though he was still in great pain.

'Now this is going to hurt, lad,' said Percy, 'but it's got to be done. We don't want to go to all this trouble then you get an infection from this slag heap.'

The private nodded. Wally put a rounded piece of wooden bite into the man's mouth to help him cope with the impending pain before he pressed down on his good shoulder to hold him firm.

Percy administered the spirit, put gauzes on the wound and bandaged them up.

The private winced and bit hard but stoically let Percy finish his job without fuss. Once done, Wally and Percy lifted the man on to their stretcher.

Wally, on his knees, checked to see if it was 'safe' to proceed and the two bearers and their 'passenger' lying on the stretcher began to move in the direction of the British trenches.

The cordite was still heavy in the air and smoke bombs to cover the advancing British troops only added to the limitation of their vision. Wally and Percy gritted their teeth and forged ahead; they had made a good forty yards when they made out a weak cry from a shallow crater.

'Wasser, wasser,' they heard.

As the bearers moved nearer, Wally, being in front, could make out a man lying prone on the ground, face up, obviously badly injured and limited in movement. A rifle lay by his side. Seeing his distinctive grey-green German uniform, Wally approached wearily.

'Wasser, Wasser, bitte,' he pleaded.

Wally's instincts told him to carry on. They already had a 'fare' and to linger much longer, he thought, would endanger their three lives. He went to move on but it was Percy who stopped him.

'Hold it, Wally. Fritz needs our help too,' he said.

'Aye,' agreed Wally, annoyed with himself that Percy should have made the humane decision and not him.

'Helfen Sie mir,' implored the German. 'Ich will nicht sterben. Bitte Gott, hilf mir.'

Wally and Percy looked at each other, neither understanding a word the man was saying.

'I think he wants some water,' said Wally, who instinctively gave a drink to the soldier who gratefully took a few large gulps.

'Danke, danke Herr,' he weakly whispered.

Percy then assessed the man's injuries. Bullets had hit him through the pelvis and just above the heart. He was in a lot of pain and the bullets had done considerable damage – one remained inside and there was a serious risk of infection if not treated soon.

He then gave him a precious nodule of morphine and did his best to dress the wounds.

'He needs a surgeon, Wally, fast. Without proper treatment he'll be dead in twenty minutes,' declared Percy.

Wally reminded Percy that they already had the British soldier to get back and they couldn't carry both of them.

'Look,' said Percy, 'let's get our bloke home and then come back for Fritz. We can't let him die here, Wally. He's somebody's son.'

Wally looked at the German who was crying in pain despite the infusion of morphine and took pity on him.

'You're right, Percy. He deserves a chance – he's the same as one of our boys in God's eyes.'

Percy and Wally then went through a charade of trying to explain what they intended to do and that they would be back for the German once they had delivered their injured soldier to safety. To reassure him, Wally left him his water bottle.

The German nodded and said, 'Danke, herren.'

Percy and Wally packed their medical kitbags and picked up the stretcher; the soldier let out a moan after being moved again. Percy nodded to the German sprawled on the ground, who was looking far more comfortable than he had five minutes before.

'Don't worry lad,' said Percy, trying to reassure the wounded Westphalian, 'we'll be back. I promise.'

The German stared at him and said nothing.

Percy turned and said to Wally, 'Come on Wally, let's get our boy to the field station.'

They had not gone but ten yards when Wally heard the distinctive crack of a rifle; the sound was still resonating in his ear when suddenly the poles of the stretcher went slack and its cargo fell, with a groan, to the ground. Wally turned around, and to his horror Percy lay with his face embedded in the mud. A hole in the back of his jacket had blood pouring out of it from the already lifeless body.

Wally looked up and saw the German with rifle in hand, pointed in his direction; for a second, one which Wally would never forget for the rest of his life, he held the stare of Percy's killer with his eyes. The German clicked the trigger but nothing came out; he then collapsed back again on the floor and moaned with pain.

Any action that Wally was considering at that time was immediately forgotten as he heard an 'Aaargh...' from the wounded British soldier at his feet. Wally knew that Percy was dead and there was nothing he could do about it but he could do something for his other comrade.

Somehow he found the strength to pick up the soldier under his good shoulder and began, with great difficulty, to drag him back toward the British lines. Any moment he expected to be shot in the back but he just kept going, determined that the man entrusted in his care would survive – a priority that he knew Percy would have insisted on.

'Come on lad, we can make it. One foot forward,' he encouraged. 'That's it son. You can do it.'

It took him a quarter of an hour to reach the British lines, his journey not made easier with the tears in his eyes and the heaviness in his heart.

'Over here, boys,' shouted two Norkies, whose trench they had

drifted to. The men came out and, much to Wally's relief, took hold of the injured Riflemen.

'Don't worry mate, we'll get him back to the Regimental Aid Post,' said one.

Wally almost fell down the parapet, exhausted by his efforts. For a few minutes he sat in silence, staring into the yonder, recalling the haunting scenes of Percy dead on his front with the gaping, bloodied hole in his back followed by the look of triumph fixed on the face of the Hun.

Wally stood bolt upright and he felt as if a stranger had taken control of his very being. At that moment Tommy and Bert came around the bend of the trench and saw their friend, standing alone, oblivious to their presence and with an unfamiliar, almost frightening look in his eyes. It was the same look that earlier that night Wally himself had witnessed in the caring soldier who had seen his friend die before picking up his rifle and seeking his vengeance; now Wally, too, was that man possessed.

'Bastard!' shouted Wally, much to the shock of Tommy and Bert who had never in their lives heard Wally swear before.

'Bastard,' he repeated with intensity. 'The murderin' Boche bastard.'

A soldier who was sitting on an upturned ammo box with his rifle leaning against the trench wall looked up in surprise at the strength of Wally's venom.

Wally appeared to snap out of his dark thoughts and grabbed the soldier's rifle.

'I'm borrowing this lad; you'll get it back, son,' he stated with an authoritative and determined voice.

The soldier got up to protest but Wally, holding in one hand the Lee Enfield, with the other hit him with a powerful punch in the solar plexus, causing him to reel backwards at speed over the box he had been sitting on and be propelled flat down onto the duckboards.

Tommy and Bert could not believe it. This was Wally, a gentle soul who detested violence in any form. They ran after him and implored him to stop, but he turned around to point the muzzle of the rifle at his two friends.

'Don't stop me, lads. I know you mean well but you're not going to stop me,' yelled Wally. 'Nobody is. There's something I have to do.'

With that he climbed over the parapet and headed towards the German trenches.

Tommy's first instinct was to go over and get his friend back but Bert quickly grabbed him by the waist and just stopped him going over the top.

'Hold it, Tommy. You did your best. I don't know what's going on in Wally's mind but you ain't going to stop him. That's Wally. There's no point in getting yourself killed, he wouldn't want that.'

Tommy slid down the wall of the trench, sighed, looked at Bert and nodded as he knew his friend was right.

Ten minutes later Wally returned and jumped back into the trench, rifle in hand.

Tommy and Bert stared at him in horror; his tunic and trousers were covered in mud and gore. Wally did not say a word but just went back to the ammo box where the soldier he punched was sitting and placed the rifle next to him, leaning it against the wall – blood dripped off its butt on to the duckboards.

Wally, as if in a world of his own, stumbled off down the trench towards the Regimental Aid Post.

Something changed in Wally Smethick forever that day. The God that he had believed in all his life had let his friend Percy die, even when, surely, he was carrying out his work and caring for the dying and wounded on both sides.

'What sort of merciful God would do that?' Wally reasoned.

That day Walter Smethick gave up on his God. However, unbeknown to Wally, his God had not given up on him!

# Chapter Fourteen

The death of Lance Corporal Percy Slaithwaite had a profound effect on Private Walter Smethick. Since the day that his fellow God fearing friend was shot in the back by the very German infantryman he was trying to save, Wally was transformed into a different man.

Maybe he was bitter and angry, Wally confessed to himself, but then again, he reasoned, he had a lot to be bitter about!

Wally Smethick was not, by nature, a violent person. Indeed, all his life he was brought up to abhor violence and confrontation and to respect those around him. He had respect for his parents, his elders, his social superiors, his preacher, his teachers, his brothers and sisters, his fellow classmates and most of all, himself.

'Love thy neighbour' was not just a tenet to be held dearly, a worthy platitude to adhere to, but it came from the lips of Jesus Christ himself, and to a devoted Christian Pacifist like Wally these were not just mere words – they were a command; a command based on love and respect for your fellow man and one which he gladly followed in his heart.

But now he was bitter that an evidently noble man like Percy Slaithwaite had been sacrificed, in his opinion, in such barbarous fashion.

'How could someone with such humane motives and obvious fraternal love for his fellow man – no matter what "side" they were on – needlessly be gunned down like that and for what? How did the loss of Percy Slaithwaite make this a better world? Did not the world need more good men like Percy to make it a richer place? Yet it seemed hell bent on destroying all that was good and sacred,' thought Wally.

Anger was not a word that could possibly adequately describe Wally's feelings at that moment, or cleanse the inner turmoil triggered by the death of his 'comrade in arms'.

If anything, he was angry with himself for believing that the God he worshipped had allowed this monstrous war to happen; a God, whom, he had been taught from an early age, had suffered crucifixion in order to bring ultimate salvation, love and peace to his fellow man.

Pondered Wally: 'Christ might have died in agony more than 1,900 years ago, strapped to a wooden cross and impaled with nails to endure a tortuous end; but where was he when Percy and thousands of others like him suffered a similar fate in the killing fields of Northern France and Belgium?'

'At least Christ had a purpose,' thought Wally, 'a message and teaching to bring man salvation from his life of sin. At least Christ knew that the agonies he endured gave hope for eternity to those who believed. At least. . .'

Wally paused and then thought of his dead friend Percy.

'What was the point of Percy's death? What possible benefit could it bring to mankind? His death would only be remembered by the few members of his loving family and his friends, until the inevitable day he faded completely from anyone's distant memory.'

Yes, he was angry. Angered by the God he loved, worshipped and trusted, who had let him and his friends down in their hour of need.

'If there was a loving God,' he queried, 'why would he let such carnage continue in this senseless war because, if he truly loved

His creation, made in his own image, then surely, with all his power and majesty He could stop such madness and self destruction in one second?'

'God,' he reasoned, 'had proved his non-existence by his inaction. Perhaps that Charles Darwin fellow was right when he said that man was nothing more than a base animal, who would stop at nothing to feed its needs and desires without consideration for his fellow creatures.

'Civilised man was just a veneer; scratch the surface and there lay a violent beast whose greed and lust knew no bounds. "Survival of the fittest," that was all that mattered; kill or be killed!' concluded Wally.

God was just a mythical being created by man himself to justify the taming of his inner beast and give some purpose and reason for his existence. Each side – British, German, French or Austrian, Russian or Turk – all claimed 'God' or 'Allah' was on their side and they were fighting in 'His name' as on a Crusade in a Holy War.

Why, didn't he once see for himself a Church of England vicar 'bless' a couple of eighteen-pounder guns on the parade ground of Moorsby Camp in front of the King's Own North Yorkshire Volunteers regiment – and even sprinkle 'holy water' over them?

'How could any church, which surely must be peace loving, bless and pay homage to a man-made piece of metal that would one day spew out its deadly cargo to rip to shreds the flesh and bones of a man born in God's image? It was purely against everything Jesus Christ himself had taught and preached. It just didn't make any sense,' thought Wally.

But it was not just God Wally was angry with. Oh no. Most of all he was angry with himself for believing in the existence of a God who could let this happen and continue to do so; a God, if he existed, that proved his weakness by not intervening, safely remaining on 'High' looking down at mankind tearing each other apart.

'What sort of loving Father would do that, who would stand

back and let his sons fight each other to death?' Wally demanded to know without finding an answer.

So that day Wally Smethick changed 'sides'. No longer would he remain a passive bystander just willing to 'pick up the pieces' and tender to the wounded and dying. He knew, deep within his being, that for years he had bottled up his natural aggression that had been chained by his genuine love of all that he previously held true and good and righteous – his Christian belief. But now his anger was channelled into a new passion, a fresh purpose to avenge the death of Percy and the many innocents like him who were needlessly slaughtered by a ruthless enemy. His new mission was 'to kill the Hun' and end this bloody war.

# Chapter Fifteen

Captain Forrester of the Lancashire Rifles was writing yet another letter of condolence – this time to the parents of one of his men who had died of his wounds the day before after taking a bullet through the head from an enemy sniper.

Though the captain was secure in a well dug out bunker on the front line of a British trench, the walls of his cavernous confines shook from the tremors of an exploding German shell fired from a howitzer which pierced the air directly above.

The light from the Hurricane lamp, which was suspended from a beam directly above Forrester's head, flickered as it swung in its cradle in response to the explosion.

A well used, off white, tarnished tin mug, which had been, before that moment, a welcome cup of tea, tumbled on the desk due to the powerful tremors, pouring liquid over an important field map before rolling on to the dirty floor.

'Blast,' swore the captain, unaware of his apt choice of words.

This and the temporary darkness disturbed the young officer's concentration and he picked up a piece of paper he was writing on and, in exasperation, screwed it up in his hand before tossing it on the ground in disgust. It was not as if the captain had not had enough practice in the last few weeks in attempting to write a personal letter of condolence to a bereaved loved one; that was bad enough at any time, but the constant interruptions made it a more onerous task for a man pushed to the limits of mental and physical capacity.

The dust caused by the vibrations whirling around the bunker began to settle, but not before many of its particles had found their way down the throat and nasal passage of the captain. Captain Forrester coughed to clear the phlegm.

His eyes diverted to a fresh piece of paper, which lay before him on the top of his makeshift desk cum mess table; the scroll was delivered twenty minutes before by a runner, and contained the latest list of battalion casualties. It did not make inspiring reading and his mood of irritation was not helped when a scruffy, short-statured private from the Royal Army Medical Corps barged unannounced into the bunker. He was followed by an equally annoyed sergeant, slightly out of breath and with his helmet askew.

'Sorry sir,' piped up the sergeant, 'this orderly asked me for permission to see you and when I refused and said you were too busy he took me unawares and pushed me out of the way. Before I knew it he had made a bolt for the door.'

Captain Forrester's gaze turned to Wally. Despite his annoyance at being interrupted, it was tempered by a puzzlement as to why this man was so keen to see him that he had 'assaulted' one of his sergeants.

'You had better have a good explanation for your conduct, private – assaulting an NCO is a serious offence. Now, man, what's so bloody important that you barge in here like this?' demanded the officer.

Before Wally could reply, Sergeant Lucas, embarrassed at being taken by surprise by the little man and his pride clearly ruffled, 'suggested' to his superior that he should not waste any more of the captain's precious time and let him take the offender outside and 'punish him' accordingly. The well-set sergeant then grabbed Wally by the arm and attempted to spin him around in one movement to swiftly eject 'the short arsed bantam' out of the door to 'sort him out'. It was a big mistake on the NCO's part. Wally, despite his diminutive size, held his footing firm and his upper body remained unmoved from the grip of an increasingly frustrated Sgt Lucas trying to move him. The bigger man, conscious that his physical efforts were embarrassingly coming to nothing in front of his captain, regained his lost balance before putting his face threateningly into Wally's – although he had to stoop down by almost a foot to do so. Sgt Lucas again grabbed Wally, this time by the lapels, but again the latter held his ground.

'Move it sonny,' he hissed. Wally remained adamant. He was not going anywhere before he could make his request to the officer. So, the smaller man, refusing to be bullied, defiantly remained rooted to the ground – much to the sergeant's annoyance.

Captain Forrester could see that neither man was going to give way, and despite telling himself that he was duty bound to punish such indiscipline by a subordinate, he could see that this uninvited intruder was serious in his intent.

The officer held up a hand to assert his authority and bring calm to the two antagonists.

'Stand down, sergeant,' he commanded, 'I want to hear what this stretcher bearer has to say. Well, lad? Don't waste my time.'

Wally, shrugging off Sgt Lucas's grip, turned to Captain Forrester, came to attention and saluted the officer.

'Permission to join your ranks, sir,' he boldly asked.

An incredulous Captain Forrester stared at Wally in disbelief.

'You want to do what, man?' he spluttered.

'Permission to become a Rifleman, sir. I want to fight,' replied Wally.

'Are you mad, man?' asked the captain. 'You are a medical orderly. A stretcher bearer for the Royal Army Medical Corps. You have been trained to tend the wounded. I thought most of you were 'Conshees'. . .'

As the officer continued, Wally stood there thinking to himself

e

he was not in the slightest offended by being labelled, even if the officer had implied it, of being a 'Conscientious Objector' – why, some of his best friends were! It was never true anyway. He was always willing to do his 'duty' but what he was not willing to do, before Percy's death, was to kill another human being...

'Now you are telling me you wish to kill the enemy. Have you taken leave of your senses, private?' queried a baffled Captain Forrester.

'No sir. In fact the very opposite, sir,' Wally retorted. 'I think I've just come to my senses. I want to be an infantryman to get back at those Boche bastards.'

Sergeant Lomas, who had thought he had seen and heard it all in his nineteen years as a regular soldier in Her and His Majesty's Forces, stood ramrod straight with a bemused expression on his face, his bushy eyebrows raised to their highest point in surprise.

Captain Forrester had heard of men in the ranks requesting to be a stretcher bearer because they thought it would be a soft option compared to the hardships of an 'ordinary soldier'. However, those requests to transfer to the RAMC never came from the front line troops who worked with the stretcher bearers because they saw for themselves, first hand, the bravery and selflessness demanded of these non-combatants, who had to deal with the gruesome sights, sounds and smells of the battlefield.

Captain Forrester made his thoughts clear.

'Look private, we have exactly sixteen stretcher bearers to cover eight hundred men in this section of the front line. You stretcher bearers play a very valuable role in this war and you can be proud that you are doing your duty. If you think for one moment that you are not doing your bit then. . .'

Wally did not let the officer finish his sentence.

'It's not that, sir,' he interrupted. 'I've seen the enemy up at close hand and in all conscience I can't stand by any longer and do nowt. Please sir, let me be a Rifleman,' Wally implored. 'I 'ave my reasons.'

'If I may be so bold, sir,' offered Sergeant Lomas. 'I've heard of soldiers volunteering to be stretcher bearers, half 'cus they think it will be a life of Riley but I've never heard a medical orderly wanting to go out and kill. Ask me sir, I think he's been sniffing too much ether.'

'Nobody asked your opinion, sergeant,' snapped an irked Captain Forrester.

The captain stood up from his makeshift desk and paced the only six steps open to him in the confines of his bunkered office.

'Now look here private. Private. . ?' he struggled to find the next word.

'What is your name, man?' he queried.

'Smethick, sir. Walter Smethick, Royal Army Medical Corps, serial number 453646, sir.' With that he again stood erect to attention and, avoiding the officer's gaze, awaited the response.

'Yes, Private Smethick,' continued Captain Forrester. The officer fixed his stare on to the crumbled sheets of condolence letters festooned on the ground.

'I suggest you go to your immediate officer in charge at the RAMC and put in your request to him first. There's a proper channel for everything in the army, private,' advised the captain.

'Respectfully, sir, I already have,' came the instant reply from Wally, 'and he said no.'

'Well, there's your reply,' quickly retorted Captain Forrester, relieved that the responsibility to make a decision was no longer his.

Much to his astonishment, however, it was not the end of the matter as far as Private Smethick was concerned.

'They refused my transfer and so 'ave you. But with all due respect, sir, it doesn't matter what anyone in this army says, I'm going to fight the Hun if it's the last thing I do in this world and nobody ain't going to stop me,' declared Wally. 'I 'ave my reasons, sir.'

With that Wally firmly fixed the eye of Captain Forrester and the officer received the message 'loud and clear' and was left in no doubt that the little stretcher bearer in front of him meant every word.

After a few seconds the captain averted Wally's disturbing but powerful gaze and his eyes looked, once again, at the screwed up bits of paper scattered at his feet before raising them to turn to the latest casualty list. Having composed himself, the officer turned on his heels and faced the wall with his back to Wally and Sergeant Lomas and stood for a few more seconds in contemplation before coming to his verdict.

'Very well, man. If you want to get yourself killed, that's your decision. I can't stop you. God knows we need more men like you with your spirit to win this ghastly war.'

'Sergeant,' barked the officer. 'Get this man transferred to our unit and get him a rifle.'

'Yes sir!' replied Sergeant Lomas, who at the same time stood to attention and saluted all in one moment – a motion that he was well drilled in. He turned to Wally.

'You are a Lancashire Rifleman now, son. It must be every Yorkshireman's dream come true to join such an esteemed regiment,' he smirked.

With that, the days of Wally's administering to the injured and dying were over, and the Christian Pacifist from Hillthorpe now had his sights on avenging the death of his friend by killing as many Germans as he could.

It might not have been what Percy wanted, but after the Boche had killed his best friend, his best friend was not here to discuss his wishes.

Or, as Wally justified to himself, in a lesson he learned from his Bible lessons and the Old Testament at Sunday School; whether you believed in a God or not, wasn't it God himself who said: 'An eye for an eye!'

# Chapter Sixteen

For the rest of his war Wally fought as an infantryman with the Lancashire Rifles. The men of his platoon first scoffed at the 'new boy' in their midst – a medical orderly turned soldier, who had never fired a gun in his life and, to some, worst of all, 'wuz a ruddy White Rose wassock with a funny accent.'

'What's e goin' to do?' offered one wit. 'Strangle Fritz with his bandages!'

'Put poison in his schnapps,' offered another.

'Smother him with a pillow,' jeered a third.

Wally didn't say a word in his own defence and refused to rise to the derision. It just made the other Lancashire Riflemen around him come to the conclusion that 'the Yorkie bantam was plain soft in the 'ead' or 'backart'.

'Shorty Yorkie' some 'christened him' behind his back; other bolder soldiers called him that straight to his face.

But Private Smethick ignored their flak and got on with the tasks assigned him. Besides, 'I'm not here to make friends,' he thought, 'but to kill Germans.'

It was not very long before the former stretcher bearer learnt to handle a Lee Enfield, and not without some aptitude and skill. Wally had a natural eye for hitting a target and it didn't go unnoticed by his NCOs. He could hit a tin can at a hundred paces and there was the odd mumble or two from the 'regular' Riflemen who could not demonstrate the same accuracy.

When their officers or sergeants asked for volunteers there were not many Lancashire Riflemen on the front line who put themselves forward – knowing that any request by their superiors for 'volunteers' usually meant the distinct opportunity of getting maimed or killed.

This did not apply to Private Walter Smethick, though. He was always the first to put his size six boot forward, especially if it decreed a chance to shoot at Fritz.

Many a time Wally would volunteer to crawl into 'No Man's Land' at night and find a decent spot to snipe at Fritz. His diminutive stature came in handy as he himself was less of a target, that and his guile and ability to blend effortlessly into the background.

The first time he shot to kill was when a young soldier, from a Saxe Coborg regiment and new to the front, decided to retrieve a football that he and his mates, in boredom, were throwing around in the trench and which had been knocked accidentally 'over the top'. Despite the pleas of his 'kamerads' the high spirited youth had not even got over the top of the ladder before a bullet hit him in the temple, killing him instantly, with his limp body sliding down the ladder and falling in a heap at its trench base.

Wally surprised himself in the lack of emotion he felt in his 'first kill'. There was no elation, no glory, no sense of achievement. He just thought of the same thing every time he pulled the trigger and 'downed' his target – and that was the sound of the gun fired by the wounded 'Boche', the groan of Percy as he fell with a bullet in his back and the sneering look on the face of his friend's murderer.

As a sniper, Wally would rarely miss the opportunity of shooting any German soldier who was foolish enough to put his head over the parapet. The Germans in turn learned very quickly not to take the risk and even cut down the numbers of patrols because of 'der Tommy Scharfschutzer'.

From then on when the Lancashire Rifles went on the offensive he was always in the thick of the action.

Time and time again his heroics amazed those all around him and the derision of his fellow platoon members eventually turned to admiration and respect.

At the Battle of Arras, in May 1917, it was Wally who single-handedly put out a well entrenched enemy machine-gun post which was causing havoc with the advancing men from Lancashire (and one Yorkshireman). With nothing but his Lee Enfield and a couple of Mills bombs, he crawled into a crater eighty yards from his target and picked off with his rifle its German defenders one by one. Following as closely, just within safety of a 'creeping barrage', courtesy of the Royal Artillery, Wally managed to get within twenty feet of the machine-gun nest. Even though the Germans were quick to replace the men who had already been felled by Wally's accurate shooting these, too, were soon dispatched with a couple of Mills bombs.

It was an action witnessed by most of his fellow Lancashire Riflemen, and not long afterwards Wally learned that he had been awarded the Military Medal for his courage on the battlefield.

His valour did not stop there. At the Battle of Passchendaele, five months later, Wally proved his worth again by saving the life of a fellow platoon member with mortar shell wounds by dragging him through the muddy bog back to his home trench for treatment. For this action a Conspicuous Gallantry Medal was added to his Military Medal.

No longer to the Lancashire Riflemen was it 'Shortie Yorkie' but 'Sergeant Smethick', who had won his battlefield spurs on merit, and woe betide any 'bloody foreigner' from any other platoon or British regiment who disrespected or 'bullragged' their little NCO!

# Chapter Seventeen

*July 16, 1916:*

'Come on Wagstaff, move it Dyson, you lazy bastards,' screamed Corporal Tilsley as he lit his Woodbine, 'you'll be the death of all of us, you miserable scum. You haven't even dug deep enough to plant a potato, let alone defend ourselves from Fritz. Put your miserable backs into it.'

Tommy and Bert picked up the pace but there was only so much energy they had after six days on a watery brew of tea, a few hard tack biscuits, the odd tin of bully beef and a few crusts of stale bread. Both grew weary, their aching limbs protesting at every shovelful.

As soon as Corporal Tilsley turned around to give his attention to his next victim in the platoon Bert poked his shovel towards the two striper's rear end – just a few feet away from its imaginary target. Sapper Dyson took great delight pretending to put the implement 'where the sun doesn't shine'.

Bert glanced at Tommy with a wide grin on his face and Tommy burst into laughter, the noise of which made the corporal instinctively swing around – only to see Bert digging more ferociously at his allotted task.

Tommy suppressed a chuckle. 'Good old Bert,' he thought,

'always wanting a laugh. What would I do without him?'

Sapper Wagstaff turned his attention back to digging his trench but the drudgery seemed just a little lighter thanks to the antics of his mate.

Corporal Tilsley surveyed the scene of the two soldiers suddenly putting the extra effort into their work. He didn't like it because he sensed they were both laughing at him but he couldn't prove it. Not that he needed proof.

'Oh by the way, Dyson,' sneered the corporal in revenge for the unknown misdemeanour, 'since you are in such a good mood I thought I'd accept your request to volunteer for tonight's point duty. That's the third night in a row you seem to have won that honour, Dyson. That could be some sort of platoon record. Well done, laddie,' and with that he cartwheeled off in another direction, laughing to himself, but loud enough for both to hear and add insult to the injury.

Any merriment Bert felt a few moments before was drained away in a second. He knew he was in for another night of torture during the coldest and darkest time. Four hours of guard duty one hundred yards closer than the rest of the platoon to the enemy lines and a potential target for any Hun sharpshooter. Four hours of biting cold, hunger, solitude and terror of not knowing whether any moment would be his last one. Bert hated Tilsley; he was a vicious little git.

Tommy could see his pal momentarily shake at another prospect 'up front'. There was no need for Tilsley to do that, he thought, not again. He could see Bert battling to hold back the tears. Tommy wasn't a vindictive man and always looked to keep the peace with his mild manner and he would never use his physical size to his advantage. This time though, even he felt an extra pang of contempt for the cocky corporal.

That night Tommy slept in the platoon trench, as near as he could to the crater where Bert was posted on point duty. Tommy tried to keep awake just in case his pal needed his help but his exhausted body won the battle and the weary sapper gratefully fell into a deep sleep – despite his resolve to keep awake. As Tommy slumbered he dreamt of his life before the war – Hillthorpe, his Dad and brothers, little Emma and most of all his Ma. All seemed so far away, even though it was barely six months since that fateful football match when he and Bert boarded the train to Hell.

Even the dust and darkness of the coalmine seemed like heaven to Tommy now – in his dreams he could smell and taste the familiar coal dust that he would breathe in every day while down the pit. What wouldn't he give now for one of Ma's hot jam cakes or a kick around with his young brothers on the 'Heap'.

His mind raced with images of home. Just for a brief, blissful moment no longer did Tommy feel the icy cold of the exposed, ruined French fields where he now found himself; no longer did the penetrating damp permeate his frozen body and, for the first time in 24 hours, even his hunger seemed no more. His body trembled as he curled up on the muddy plank dug into the wall of the trench but Sapper Wagstaff was not aware of his physical actions as he slept. Instinctively his arms hugged themselves around his Lee Enfield rifle and the discomfort of his lumpy kitbag for a pillow was soon forgotten in his slumbering state.

It was not long before his happy 'sleep' was interrupted by a faint voice coming from above the parapet of the trench.

'Tommy, Tommy, I'm coming in,' whispered a weak but familiar voice.

'Bert,' whispered Tommy as loudly as he dared, 'is that you?'

'Dyson, Albert, King's Own North Yorkshire Volunteers,' came back the reply in an almost inaudible but nevertheless, desperate reply. Normally Bert would have made a little quip to make Tommy grin, even in the darkest moment, but this time there was no touch of humour, no laughter in the voice.

Tommy, who by now was on his feet and relieved to hear the familiar voice of his pal, caught a pair of almost inhuman eyes looking down upon him from the parapet of the trench as Bert crawled back to the 'safety' of the British lines through the thick, unrelenting mud. However, the eyes that met Tommy looked as though they were not of a soul from this world and spoke of fear and desperation and physical torment – a look that would haunt Tommy for many years to come.

'You made it Bert,' exclaimed Tommy, relieved that his mate's ghastly ordeal was over. 'Give me a jiffy and I'll brew you a cuppa.'

Bert didn't, or couldn't, reply but looked towards Tommy to acknowledge his presence. He clearly didn't have the strength at that moment and his frozen body trembled with cold. Tommy wrapped a field blanket around the soldier's shoulders to try and thaw out his friend and soon realised that any attempt at any sort of conversation was useless.

Bert just gazed into the void before him and began to shiver violently, his uniform soaked through from lying half in a crater puddle all night, while the 'drier' half was saturated with the morning dew of dawn to add to his misery. Having crawled both to and from the forward observation post, every fibre of his uniform was filthy and earthy in colour and having blacked himself up to help camouflage his movement, Bert was not going to pass any parade muster for smartness.

'You did it mate,' encouraged Tommy, trying to appeal to Bert's sense of bravado and adventure. 'You survived. I knew you would, you got more guts than me Bert Dyson, that's for sure.'

Although these words were meant to cheer his mate up they not did evoke the response Tommy had hoped for. Bert just sat there staring and shivering and then he began to sob. It was as if his whole being was saying 'no, no more'.

Tommy didn't say a word but he knew – he knew his friend was not a coward, he had seen that these last few months as they shared the torment of trench warfare together. Tommy remembered that the man before him now was the same Bert who had helped pull him from the rubble to save his life when they were boys at Hillthorpe Colliery.

It was the same Bert who, with his little jokes and optimism, had helped Tommy keep his own sanity during the last six months, all the way through the training on the bleak Yorkshire moors and more so in the past few months in the hell of the front line. It was also the same man who had saved his life from the thrust of a German bayonet.

'Come on mate, they won't let you into the snug at the Collier's Arms dressed like that,' offered Tommy – trying the same humorous tactics which Bert always used on him successfully when he was down. On this occasion even humour could not penetrate his friend's fragile state of mind and body, and Bert fell to his knees in despair, like a wounded animal about to die.

At that very moment Corporal Tilsley emerged from around the corner of the trench, dressed immaculately as only corporals can be at first light in the morning.

'Bastard,' thought Tommy. 'He's just been preparing himself for this very moment and made sure he was awake to "welcome" Bert back from his point duty.'

'Dyson, you miserable little turd, what the hell do you think you're doing? You still have three minutes of watch to do on my reckoning. Why aren't you at your post? Look at you, you miserable excuse for a soldier,' barked Tilsley.

'Stop whimpering like a Jesse and clean yourself up. You ought to thank me for not putting you on a charge of deserting your post. Now get back over there and don't come back for another two hours. Move it.'

As he stood over his trembling victim, the corporal stood above Bert and kicked him up the backside when he could not elicit any response. Bert, who had lain there, blank in expression and too frozen to move, suddenly dragged himself from the ground and onto his knees before going into, what appeared from all the symptoms, an epileptic fit. At this Tilsley, in both a mixture of fury and delight, kicked him once more and then dragged the unfortunate soldier by his lapels and lifted him to his feet – intending to knock more 'sense' into Bert.

'Move it, you miserable little coward,' snarled Tilsley as he pushed Bert up against the wall of the trench. 'You think I'm going to let you skive off and shirk your duty,' barked the corporal, who took off the rifle around his shoulder at the same time as giving Bert another kick. He took the rifle in two hands and raised it to use the butt on his hapless victim.

All this was too much for Tommy, who until that moment stood watching, his anger rising as he witnessed the corporal dishing out such unfair and vicious abuse on his best pal. Tommy instinctively dived in and punched Tilsley smack in the mouth, sending him reeling against the duckboards of the trench floor before he rolled again with a splash into a pool of foetid water.

Tommy stood upright, waiting for any sort of response from the hated little corporal.

'One more move,' shouted the normally placid Tommy in a dark and threatening voice that came from deep within him. 'One more move and I'll bloody kill yer.'

'I'll have you Wagstaff, I'll have you,' whined Tilsley, who tried to justify himself with some sort of dignified response, but soon realised the futility as Tommy came towards him to land another blow. Now it was Tilsley's turn to 'cry like a Jesse' and the bully now found himself as the victim and realised he had gone an insult too far.

As Tommy raised his fist and Tilsley cowered and begged for forgiveness to avert the impending blow, a noise like an express train hurtled towards them. There was an enormous boom and it was as if the entire world itself was blown to smithereens when a German shell exploded above the trench. Tommy found himself flying through the air as if the ground beneath his feet was sucked from under him.

Everything appeared to go into slow motion before he hit the ground again with a thud some ten yards from where he previously stood above Tilsley. The shock and impact of his landing knocked the wind out of his body before he momentarily lost consciousness.

A few minutes later he regained his senses. He opened his eyes. It was a great relief to know he could see. He began to choke through a combination of the mud he had swallowed pushing against the vomit which was trying to force its way out in the opposite direction. His ears rang from the vibration of the explosion and his focus was unsteady. Soon the ringing in his ears began to fade, his focus returned and instinctively he felt with his right hand to make sure all his limbs were intact. To his immense relief they were and he said a silent prayer to himself of thanks. Despite the pain that racked his body from the shock of the blast, he felt the euphoria of just knowing he was still alive. Life at that moment never felt to Tommy so precious.

He gathered himself, raising his weary torso first to his knees and then to his feet. His aching body protested with every movement and it seemed as if Tommy had been burdened with a hundredweight tied to each limb. Tommy, now almost erect, looked ten yards to his left. There lay Corporal Tilsley, sitting in the same position he was just before the blast. Ironically it was the protection from Tommy's body, as he towered over him to thump the two-striper, that had shielded the corporal from the worst of the explosion and undoubtedly saved his life.

Tilsley sat bolt upright. His body was stiff – it was as if he had heard the order 'officer on parade' and instinctively stood to attention while in a sitting position. This time, Tommy noticed, there was not the usual cruel, weasel-like expression but Tilsley's face was ashen and corpse-like with a fixed stare looking at nowhere, his mind not in the moment.

Tilsley was alive but Tommy's thoughts were not about the corporal's immediate well being, his only concern was for Bert.

'Bert, Bert, where are you mate?' screamed Tommy in a voice that even its owner could not recognise, which like the rest of his body had not yet recovered from the trauma of the last few minutes.

Tommy, still giddy and struggling to take in the circumstances in which he now found himself, looked around frantically but could not see his pal. He couldn't understand, where was he? He was only here a few moments ago, Tommy thought.

That second he looked to his right and the full horror of war suddenly struck him with more force than any exploding shell could muster. There, on the ground just a few yards from where Tommy stood, lay a human arm, detached from the rest of its owner's torso.

Tommy staggered slowly towards the gruesome object and he sensed a horrific foreboding – as he got closer all his worst fears began to be realised. Tommy could see clearly that the limb was still perfectly intact and the uniform, which had just previously adorned it, now had mere shreds of cloth clinging to it. The whole arm still smouldered from the heat of the blast. Further inspection resulted in Tommy recognising the shoulder badge of his regiment on one of the fragments. He knew the limb belonged to Bert; there was no one else it could be. To torment him even further, he soon discovered more parts of Bert's body scattered around the battlefield.

A torrent of anguish, that first appeared to emanate from the pit of his stomach, seemed to explode inside him and a wave of utter despair smothered him like a damp, heavy blanket. He sank to his knees and let out an almost inhuman cry which pierced the dawn, to all who heard it, like no other sound that could elicit such human misery.

# Chapter Eighteen

Following the five minute barrage by the German guns the deadly salvo of howitzer fire suddenly ceased and once again a peaceful, yet eerie silence fell upon the front. It was as if an erupting volcano had finished spewing fiery larva from its loins and all that remained was the discharge of its ashes, choking the atmosphere. The acrid smell of cordite hung in the air over the trenches and only the cries of the wounded and broken could now be heard.

Sergeant Howie of the King's Own North Yorkshire Volunteers was the first NCO on the scene to inspect the damage caused by the enemy shelling. It was his job to report the number of casualties, sort out the evacuation of the wounded and assess and organise the repair of the defences.

His party soon found Corporal Tilsley. It was as if a corpse sat upright on the floor but this 'corpse' was very much alive. Only the outer shell looked perfectly preserved, no marks on the outer body but when it came to the man himself there appeared to be nobody 'at home'. The explosion may not have left any physical damage on the despised NCO but his mind was 'blown' and no longer was he the 'cocky corporal'.

'Looks like the war's over for you, son,' said the tall, blond sergeant, but Tilsley was in no condition to answer. Two burly soldiers took him away and Sgt Howie and two of his squad moved onto the next man.

He found Sapper Tommy Wagstaff nearby on the floor of the forward trench, knees up against his chest, arms clutching his head and rocking slowly. Sgt Howie bent down and gently touched Tommy on the shoulder but the rocking continued.

'Come on, son,' whispered the sergeant. 'It's all over now.'

There was still no response, so the NCO shook Tommy a little more and dragged the shell-shocked sapper to his feet.

Tommy, his face chalk white in pallor, was unable to stand by himself without the support of his fellow soldiers; he began to gasp for breath.

'Come on sapper, pull yourself together, it's over now,' said one of the privates.

'Poor bastard,' confided the sergeant to his men in a low voice so Tommy could not hear, 'looks like another one's lost it.'

Sgt Howie had seen many victims of the war, far too many for his liking, in his eighteen months on the front lines.

'That poor lad has not got a mark on him, but he'll never be the same again,' thought the battle hardened sergeant. 'He's only just a boy, poor sod. What had the lad done to see his mates blown up like that, or any of them for that matter?'

Sgt Howie picked up Tommy's rifle, and put it around the shaking sapper's shoulders. He knew that if the man in front of him reported back without his rifle there was even a chance that he would be put on a serious charge if he came up before an over-zealous officer determined to show the ranks 'how to conduct themselves properly'. The NCO knew of cases where front line soldiers who had endured days of continuous shelling had finally 'cracked' under the strain, only to be written off by the medical officer as suffering from LMF – Lacking Moral Fibre.

'Take him back lads,' ordered Howie. The two privates started to lead Tommy back along the trench to join Corporal Tilsley, who was now safely back at the medical station.

'No, no,' screamed Tommy, finally finding his voice, 'I must find Bert. I must find Bert.'

Tommy tried to push away his minders in frustration but the escorts stiffened their grip on their 'invalid'. It only served to make Tommy more agitated and this time the sympathetic sergeant raised his voice to underline his authority.

'Get back to the MO, sapper, and that's an order,' barked Howie.

Suddenly Tommy, who since the explosion had lost all sense of reality and any control of his physical actions, now became more focused and lucid.

'I must find Bert,' he repeated. 'I won't go until I've found him.'

'Who's Bert?' asked the sergeant looking at the men standing on each side of Tommy.

'It's his best mate sir,' replied Sapper Harris, who was in the same platoon as the two pals and was himself from Hillthorpe.

'I'm afraid he's gone, son,' said Sgt Howie softly to Tommy, trying to break the news with the minimum of impact.

'I'm not going until I've found Bert,' cried Tommy. 'I'm not stupid, I know he's dead but I've got to find him and put him to rest. I owe him that much.'

Sgt Howie looked into Tommy's eyes and saw the determination – no longer was he staring at a lost soul but a soldier with purpose. No longer did he see a frightened animal, who shortly before rocked at his feet.

'Please sir, let me bury him. We joined up together,' pleaded Tommy.

The sergeant, not a man used to having his orders questioned, relented to the request and nodded his head to give approval.

'If the young fool wants to bury his pal then why should I stop him,' thought Howie. 'He'll only get one chance and the army owes him that much after what he's been through.'

Tommy went to pick up a nearby shovel left in the trench and Howie put out an arm to stop him.

'You know he's been blown to bits son, it won't be pretty,' said the sergeant.

'Yes sir,' mumbled Tommy, 'I do.'

'Alright soldier, do what you have to do and be quick about it,' ordered Sgt Howie in a firmer voice, 'and make sure you keep your head down. I don't want more men lost today.'

The sergeant and his two privates continued on their inspection and left Sapper Wagstaff to continue his grisly task.

# Chapter Nineteen

Where he got the strength from that day Tommy didn't know, but it was as if an inner force guided him in the task he had chosen to undertake. It was something instinctive – he just knew his 'duty' and got on with it.

He picked up the shovel, gathered a few blankets to make some sacking, and began the gruesome deed of collecting the scattered remnants of Bert's mutilated body. Tommy picked up the piece of arm first and placed it on the woollen blanket. A few yards further he found a piece of thigh, covered in gore and twisted at an unnatural angle – that, too, he gently added to the hideous pile, but Tommy no longer felt shock or repulsion.

He didn't even want to think, he couldn't afford to – all Tommy was focused on was collecting as much of his friend as possible. It wasn't long before he found a jagged piece of skull lying face down in the mud. Parts of the brain were still visible and matted with blood and gore. He placed it with the rest of the macabre collection and gently wrapped it up into a bundle. The total sum of his endeavours bore no resemblance at all to his closest mate. It didn't matter, Tommy knew it was Bert and that was all he cared about. He was determined to give Bert Dyson a decent burial – maybe not a proper Christian one, but at least

Tommy could mark his friend's grave at the place where he so valiantly fought and died.

Sapper Tommy Wagstaff picked up the bundle and his new job began. He first looked for somewhere to dig the grave. Just in front of the forward trench, and maybe twenty yards from where the deadly explosion took place, Tommy found his spot.

All around the battlefield, which was once, only two years before, a field rich in golden corn, lay a desolate, barren, unforgiving landscape – swamped by a sea of mud, bomb craters and barbed wire.

Sapper Wagstaff, now armed with a commandeered pick and shovel tied to his back and carrying the precious remains, saw a solitary poppy flower clinging defiantly for life among the ravaged landscape. Apart from the remains of a few stubborn wooden stumps, which had long since lost the rest of their trees to the incessant shelling, the little poppy was the only surviving plant-life within sight of Tommy's trench. The distinctive red flower looked sad, withered and alone but to Tommy, at that moment, it was the most beautiful thing he had seen in the past six months. Respectfully he put down the bundle, along with his tools, and picked up a short piece of splintered wood – no doubt blown across the field from the remains of planks shoring up a field trench.

He drew his bayonet, sat down, oblivious to his surroundings, and sawed the plank into two before concentrating on one piece and etching out the name of his friend – 'Sapper Bert Dyson KONYV'.

Beside the little poppy Tommy began to dig.

Many of his fellow Norkies shouted at him from the back of the trench as the Germans continued the shelling of the British lines.

'Get back here, you bloody idiot,' shouted Corporal Allerdyce, who was joined in his anxiety by several other soldiers. 'You'll get yourself killed.'

Tommy kept on digging.

'Wagstaff, what the hell do you think you're doing? Now get your arse over here now,' ordered Corporal Allerdyce, who was more concerned that every Fritz gunner for miles would be homing in on their position because of that 'bloody loony Sapper Wagstaff'.

Tommy ignored Corporal Allerdyce and he ignored Lieutenant Bowyer, much to the officer's annoyance. He also ignored the German guns and the real danger of the German snipers, who could have taken his life at any moment. He just kept on digging.

Tommy marked out the grave carefully with the little red poppy at its head – and dug. Where he found the renewed energy from after the battering he had just undertaken, he could not explain.

As he dug he thought of Bert and the times they had laughed together, both in the pits and more recently during their shared life in the army. Tommy thought of Bert's Ma and Da at Daleswick; how would they cope without their only beloved son, snatched away from them, and for what? A piece of Froggie mud in No Man's Land! How could he face them if he ever went home? Would he ever see his own family again? What would his Ma say? How could he look her in the eye after betraying her and running off to join up? His mind was in turmoil.

The soft earth was easy to shovel but Tommy felt a sudden heaviness as he began to realise he would never see his best mate again. He looked up and saw the little poppy at the top of the half dug grave flutter in the wind and rain, its petals looking as if they were ready to break away from its stem at any second and be blown away forever by the elements.

As he worked, the war continued around him. Although the shelling was not so intense there were sporadic explosions along the long trenches; the odd burst of machine-gun fire and the crack of rifle shot which reminded both sides of the other's presence. Throughout, Tommy continued and Corporal Allerdyce and Lieutenant Bowyer checked the progress of the stubborn sapper through a field periscope.

'He's a lucky bugger,' thought the corporal. 'He should be in that grave himself with all those whizz-bangs.'

But Tommy was not aware of the war going on around him; his only interest was the task in hand. It was as if, at that moment, he had no sense of danger. Strangely, and it certainly appeared to be true for the men of the King's Own North Yorkshire Volunteers crouching for their lives in the forward trench, Sapper Wagstaff's little spot on the French field seemed to be the safest place of all on the front. With fire now steadily increasing again along the front line, no shell, mortar or bullet came within fifty feet of where Tommy prepared his friend's grave.

It was as if the Germans could sense that here was a man doing his duty to his comrade and they had no earthly right to disturb the mad English Tommy in his humanitarian task – a deed they themselves could relate to in this mad, mad war.

Tommy dug and he dug deep. He was used to wielding a pick and shovel – it was a natural talent – honed by his years in the pits and by the ample opportunities for the back breaking task offered courtesy of His Majesty's Armed Forces.

The sapper got into his natural rhythm with hand, shoulders and brain all working in harmonious unison. He knew exactly what he had to do – how deep, how wide, and how long. Soon the death pit began to take shape and even though Tommy possessed only a few, precious fragments of Bert's remains he dug the grave to the true proportions befitting his friend, as he remembered him that morning before the tragic explosion.

With the back of the blade Tommy pounded the sides of the grave, taking care that each wall of the pit was neat and smooth. Satisfied that all was in order, Tommy climbed out of the hole and picked up the pathetic bundle of human remains.

As he looked down at the grey army issue blanket cupped in his hands, Tommy stood quite still. He remembered the anguished face of Bert peering at him from the other side of the trench earlier that fateful morning. He recalled a face looking scared and helpless; it was not the familiar one of man or boy

119

he knew – the face always full of life and with a cheeky smile.

'There's not much laughter in war,' thought Tommy.

All around him the howitzers pounded, the machine-guns rattled and the earth trembled but Tommy did not care, he was fighting other battles.

He placed the bundle beside the grave, jumped into the pit and reached up to tenderly place the remains of his friend into its final resting place – carefully putting the remnants in to some sort of order that befitted its owner's body in life as best as he could. Then Tommy stood for a minute, uttering a prayer known only to him and his Maker, before climbing out.

Again the soldiers of the King's Own North Yorkshire Volunteers shouted at 'Mad Tommy' to come back into the relative safety of their trench – but 'Mad Tommy' wasn't listening. As his fellow soldiers looked on in wonder and disbelief, Tommy began the laborious task of back shovelling to fill in the grave he had just so freshly dug. To anyone else this task would have been arduous, and in the circumstances it was one of reckless madness, but to Sapper Wagstaff this simple act was his duty to a friend and comrade in arms.

When the last part of the clammy, dirty brown soil was returned to fill Bert's grave Tommy put down his shovel. It was then he took his roughly made cross and knocked it into the earth just behind the little flower.

His eyes gazed at the little red poppy that fluttered in the fierce, biting north easterly wind. He then stood erect to attention and saluted his fallen comrade.

This simple act was witnessed by friend and foe alike, but of the hundreds of men who were privileged to see this rare act of humanity in a place many thought God had surely abandoned – it was a sight they would never forget.

Lieutenant Bowyer's jaw dropped as he watched in amazement through his field glasses.

'Corporal, who's that man standing next to that bloody idiot saluting in No Man's Land?' barked Bowyer.

f

Corporal Allerdyce squinted his one eye and looked through the field periscope at Sapper Wagstaff, who he could see with his back to him and making a salute to his fallen comrade.

'What man, sir?' said a puzzled Allerdyce. 'I don't see anybody but Sapper Wagstaff.'

That tall man, standing right over him, the one with the long flowing red hair and the bright, white uniform. You can't miss him! What's the matter corporal, are you blind, man?'

'No, sir, with respect, sir, I don't know what you're talking about. There's only Wagstaff sir, nobody else would be that stupid to be out there, sir.'

'Good God man,' expounded Lieutenant Bowyer. 'Am I surrounded by blithering idiots? Of course there's another soldier with him, I've never seen a man with such long, flaming red hair. Whoever that soldier is, corporal, tell him to get his bloody hair cut,' snapped the officer in the plummiest of British upper class accents.

'Blimmin' officers,' muttered Corporal Allerdyce, in a less reverential tone, facing away from the irate lieutenant, 'Wassocks, all of 'em.'

# Chapter Twenty

Throughout the rest of the war Tommy had now found his purpose. Burying Bert was the first of many victims that the Yorkshireman committed to the earth. Hundreds upon hundreds of bodies belonging to men in the prime of their life, some whole but most gruesomely dismembered, were entrusted to the care of Sapper Wagstaff. Each one was special to Tommy, who knew each was precious to someone, and had shared a similar hellish experience to himself.

Mostly the corpses were laid out in rows of twenties – similarly covered with a khaki canvas. Tommy, who had volunteered to perform burial duties, along with some poor unfortunate fellows who were ordered to perform the grisly task, soon became used to the sad, pathetic sight of the twisted and shattered cadavers, but not one of them ever could get used to, or indeed would ever forget, the sweet pungent reek of death that permeated the air with more force than any cordite shell.

Sapper Tommy Wagstaff had a bit of a reputation as a loner in his unit. It wasn't that Tommy meant to be unsociable. Tommy knew he was never one of the lads, he wasn't that interested – he had joined up with Bert and they had stuck together and just got on with whatever the army, and even Corporal Tilsley, had to throw at them.

Tommy was 'a big bugger' who didn't do them any harm so the 'lads' in the platoon just left him and Bert alone.

When his best mate had died, Tommy wasn't concerned about making new friends. In his mind he had already seen his boyhood pal blown to smithereens in front of his eyes – there was only one Bert.

'What was the point of making friends anyway,' reasoned Tommy, 'if the next day they could be dead with a bullet or a piece of shrapnel through their skull? If you don't make friends you won't feel so bad when they die! Perfectly logical.' So Tommy kept to himself. Nothing personal.

# Chapter Twenty-one

The eleventh hour of the eleventh day of the eleventh month, 1918. All around the Western Front the guns fell silent. For hundreds of thousands of men on both sides the war in the wasted fields of France and Belgium had ended, but the battles in their heads and souls continued to rage – and for most no earthly peace would reign again in their lifetime.

No soldiers fortunate enough to 'survive' the bloody carnage with limbs intact, who participated in the orgy of inhumanity between the 'civilised' nations of Europe, would ever be the same again. The boy or man who first enlisted, or was conscripted, to fight for 'King or Emperor and Country' was not the same person after being spewed out by the Great War when the shattered nations laid down their arms.

There was no hero's welcome for our Tommy; no victorious parade of smartly marching troops greeted with bunting and drum and trumpet; no adoring females and grateful menfolk to express their eternal gratitude – such as Tommy remembered that fateful day many lifetimes ago when he proudly made his mark and enlisted on Hillthorpe playing fields.

No, for Tommy there was just more work to do, more earth to dig, more bodies to intern; more young, wasted lives to salute goodbye, although Tommy liked to think more in terms of a phrase he had picked up on his Continental 'journey' – 'au revoir'.

Despite the fact that 'The Great War to end all Wars' had officially ended in November, 1918, it was, for thousands of British soldiers who volunteered or were conscripted, the dream of returning to Blighty, their homes and loved ones, that really mattered, and this was cruelly delayed by their 'superiors' who had a different agenda to fulfil.

As politicians of all nations prepared to gather at the Palace of Versailles outside Paris to pick out the spoils of the rotten carcass of those nations deemed 'responsible' – ie the losers – Sapper Wagstaff remained in Flanders.

There were many 'survivors' like him now – fit of body but shattered in mind; no visible marks on the surface, but these unfortunate men were a shell of the boy/man that they used to be. Inside Tommy felt a weariness beyond his tender years – strangely when he looked in the shaving mirror he saw the face of his Da staring right back with the eyes and face sunken like the roof of a broken mine shaft.

Although there was no logical reason why he should blame himself he was increasingly burdened down with a sense of guilt – the guilt of the survivor who is weighed down with the curse that he is alive while thousands, and even millions, like his pal Bert, had been brutally killed. And for what?

Every day, every minute, every second and in every breath, Tommy could not escape the turmoil in his mind – it was like he was battling on a front against an overwhelming force of infinite power – no matter what he did, where he was, nothing could wrench away the pain of his experience. He was not alone; there were thousands of men like him, on both sides – just another soldier who would have to 'get on with it' – returning to a society which could never fully understand – not that many wished to – their pitiable plight.

While he was in uniform Tommy found he could cope. He still

had the flashbacks, especially at night when he awoke, screaming, with the images of Corporal Tilsley, sitting bolt upright in ghostly form, or Bert's face staring back at him so hauntingly when he crawled back to the trench just before he was blasted to death. Although Tommy's cries awoke the other soldiers in the damp, cold Belgium barn that served as their barracks, there were no complaints – because they all had nightmares of their own.

# Chapter Twenty-two

*December 14, 1918:*

One month after silence reigned for the first time on the Western Front in four years, the legacy of 'man's inhumanity to man' still lay strewn in the killing fields of Flanders and Northern France.

What before the war were lands of mostly corn blessed fields and ancient, picturesque towns and villages was now completely unrecognisable from its original form – hideously transformed into a barren wasteland, its devastation equal to anything that Nature itself could marshal its most terrible forces to have caused.

Tens of thousands of human bodies and horses were laid down in its desecrated soil, twisted in a myriad of contorted shapes, cast down as if by an enormous hand belonging to a gigantic farmer, who, striding across the countryside, had scattered their corpses across the fields, like seeds of corn to sow which now bore a gruesome harvest.

Private Tommy Wagstaff was now officially part of a Pioneer Corps unit whose job was to 'recover' the dead and bring some order to the chaos of the human carnage that remained untouched on the battlefields. He, with hundreds of other British and Allied soldiers, was given the grisly task of finding the dead, bagging anything that would help identify its owner – such as a dog tag, identity card or personal possessions – recording the contents, then bringing the body back to a central point for a place of burial.

Sergeant Dann informed Tommy that those 'collected' would be buried in a mass grave until a later date, when they would be exhumed and a 'proper' cemetery could be built to give them a final and more dignified 'resting place'.

Even in death the soldiers were divided mostly into different 'trenches' depending on the country they fought for or if they were officer or rank.

The men allotted this gruesome task were a disparate collection – volunteers, like Tommy, or those press ganged into service due to some misdemeanour. The latter would have preferred life in the British Army's most inhospitable glasshouse rather than this grizzly duty – but they had no choice.

They were joined by more than one hundred and forty reluctant German prisoners of war.

The High Command's philosophy, this time echoed by the lower ranks in the British Army, was that 'the bloody Krauts started this mess, and they can bloody well clear it up.'

Besides the awful stench and the sweet odour of rottenness that permeated the air all around, the sights that greeted the men who performed the unenviable job were not for the faint-hearted. The bodies, in various stages of decomposition, were carrion for birds, foxes, rats and other wild animals, while maggots and other worm life gorged on the plentiful feast. Many were not intact in limb or head, and like Bert, blasted to 'Kingdom Come'.

For some it was too much to bear, and many a man on the 'burial party' had to be replaced having 'flipped over the edge' or 'Lost His Moral Fibre' as one unsympathetic officer opined.

But for Tommy it was not an onerous task to be feared or revolted by as it was for so many of the men around him. No, to him, it was his duty to those who had died in this brutal war, no matter which side they were on, it was a chance to give the poor souls a dignified, Christian burial. It would, he thought, at least give those who loved them the knowledge that someone, somewhere had cared enough to take the trouble to give them a respectable final resting place alongside those they had fought and died with.

For his fellow 'workers' it was a horrendous but necessary task; dignity to the dead soldier did not come into it – 'get the job done as quickly as possible, pile them up and on to the next'. However, to Tommy each corpse he handled was 'special' because he knew that each one had been through their own personal hell and he accorded them their due and deserved respect.

Despite his liking for working on his own, carting bodies around was not a one man job and whether he liked it or not he was 'assigned' a German POW to help with his chores.

Tommy tried to shrug off his 'accomplice' but Corporal Siegfried Muller, a red-headed man aged in his mid-twenties, of average height but stocky, muscular build, was not to be deterred.

Although language was a barrier – Tommy spoke no German and the German no English – somehow they, in time, began to understand each other's needs. Even in their break times Tommy just sat in complete silence and the more animated Siegfried soon learned to do the same and await his 'orders'.

When the work was done for the day, each would go back to their own quarters – Tommy a commandeered farm where he slept in a barn with thirty other British soldiers; Siegfried back to the tent in a hastily erected POW compound, surrounded by barbed wire, watch towers and guards.

When the 'death squads' worked – as they soon became known by the troops – they were guarded by armed men, on the lookout for any looting, with orders to shoot – especially at POWs trying to escape. At the end of the day, the men were searched to make sure that they had not 'acquired' any souvenirs from their 'customers'. It was instant Court Martial for those who did and a firing squad for any 'thieving Boche'.

Over the weeks Tommy became use to Siegfried and the latter soon grew to respect 'Die großen Tommy' who, although he did not say much, treated him well. Tommy gave him some of his rations – of biscuits, bread, jam, bully beef or a mug of tea – something that the man was mightily grateful for and a much needed supplement to his own sparse POW entitlement.

Siegfried observed the way Tommy would take care to handle each dead soldier in whatever state he was found, with thought and consideration. Every small detail was meticulously recorded and any found article carefully bagged; each corpse was put on to a stretcher and carried with utmost respect, as if its owner was still of this world. Even those whose remains were scattered were accorded the same consideration – just like he did with Bert.

During the next few weeks the pair worked in silent harmony, extracting hundreds of bodies from the foetid fields of war – and Siegfried soon began to share his English workmate's ethos of doing his duty in honouring the fallen.

Although they did not talk very much, Tommy and Siegfried soon discovered that they had something in common, for the German from the Ruhr Valley was a coal miner before the war. In fact, one day, while the pair were joining twenty other men digging out a burial pit for two hundred and five dead soldiers from the Warwickshire Warriors, Siegfried 'told Tommy off' for not 'digging properly' – an action he demonstrated by taking the Englishman's shovel and giving him a lesson on how to do it the right way – 'German style'.

For the first time in many months Tommy smiled, amused at the way his work companion handled the shovel. When Siegfried picked up his own tool and started to dig, Tommy grabbed it from him, shook his head in mock disapproval, and returned the compliment – 'English style'!

'This is 'ow we do it in England,' beamed Tommy, and they both laughed – still not understanding a word they were saying to each other.

For a moment Tommy remembered when he and Bert joked about sticking the shovel 'where the sun don't shine' up Corporal Tilsley.

Then, as soon as he thought of Bert, his good spirits evaporated and he turned his back on Siegfried and resumed his digging – purposely moving a good few yards away to be alone.

Later that morning Siegfried approached Tommy, who was taking a well earned few minutes rest, sitting on an abandoned gun carriage rendered useless by a mortar shell.

'Tommy,' implored the German, 'Schauen Sie sich das an. Bitte,' and stretched out his hand to offer Tommy a small, and crumpled black and white photograph.

Tommy took the photograph and looked at it. There was a squat, muscular Siegfried standing with the unease that would be felt by any hard working miner, used to dirt and sweat most of his life, finding himself forced to squeeze himself into his only 'Sunday' suit, worn for the family photograph. He was surrounded by a plump and happy flaxen-haired Mrs Siegfried and their two little children, a boy and a girl, aged about six and seven – well proportioned little cherubs.

'Helga,' Siegfried said, pointing to his wife, followed by 'Mannfred, Gretchen,' indicating his children.

Tommy stared at the photograph and Siegfried felt a little pride in showing his English friend his most precious possession, but his pride soon turned to shock when Tommy just thrust the photograph back and ran away.

'Tommy, Tommy, was ist das. . ?' queried a puzzled Siegfried, but Tommy just got up and ran away, wanting to find anywhere else, just to be alone.

Siegfred stood in puzzlement, not knowing what had come over the Englishman. He thought he was his friend.

When Tommy found a quiet spot by himself he hated himself for his sudden show of emotion. He didn't mean to be rude to the amiable German but seeing the little photograph just reminded Tommy of his own family at Hillthorpe – Ma and Da, Edward and Victor and little Emma – everything he had missed over these last few years – and it was too much for him to bear.

*　　*　　*　　*

The next day it was pouring down with rain on a bleak, cold winter's day as the 'death squad' prepared to start their work.

Tommy went over to Siegfried and tried to apologise for his outburst, but despite the language barrier between the two, words were not necessary. Tommy gave Siegfried the last of his daily bread ration, but the latter refused it, shaking his head and smiling as if to tell the former, 'there was no need – he was forgiven.'

Tommy broke the bread in two and again offered a piece to his friend and this time Siegfried accepted it. They washed down their food with a bottle of red wine that somehow Siegfried had managed to secrete in his trench coat.

Two hours later Tommy was summoned by Sergeant Dann for his next burial task. Siegfried waited a few respectful yards away, ready for instructions once his English 'boss' had received his orders.

Sergeant Dann pointed out to Tommy a ridge about two hundred yards away that he wanted cleared of dead bodies by the end of the day.

'There's a platoon of dead Lancashire Riflemen in there but you will find scores of dead Hun as well. The Lancs charged the German trench. Brave sods, they were up against a crack Prussian unit. There was some real vicious fighting there, hand to hand stuff. Poor bastards fighting and dying like that. I was told it took place on November 8, just three days before the Armistice. Bloody tragedy. Poor sods. I doubt they would have moved out of their trenches if they knew,' said the chatty sergeant.

'After the battle, the trench caved in as the artillery fire crept up and blew it to smithereens. Our lads have been clearing it for the last couple of days and I want you to give them a hand.'

'Did you say, Lancashire Rifles, Sergeant?' asked Tommy.

'Yes, that's right,' came the reply. 'Why, did you know them lad?'

Tommy nodded and said: 'I knew one of them, 'e wuz a mate of mine. Wally. . . I mean Private Walter Smethick.'

Despite the now heavy rain Sergeant Dann looked down at his

clipboard, where he had a list of names which could tally with the British dead on the ridge.

He scrolled down the list and shook his head.

'No, there's no Private Walter Smethick here,' he said, before turning the page.

Tommy let out a sigh of relief.

'Wait a minute. Here it is, Sergeant Walter Smethick. Aye lad, that's him.'

The sergeant rubbed his chin in thought.

Tommy stood motionless with shock and a wave of despair came over him.

'No, not Wally. Not him as well. God no,' he cried inside to himself.

Sergeant Dann, oblivious to Tommy's sudden grief, continued, eager to pass on information to a friend of the deceased.

'I've heard of him. Sergeant Walter Smethick. He was a right little Jack Russell. The lads found his body with about five bullets in him and a bayonet thrust. He went down fighting, that lad, his corpse was surrounded by five dead Prussians, all six-footers. That Sergeant Smethick was as brave as they come. I heard he led the charge himself when the officers were mowed down and all the Lancs piled in after him. They took the trench but lost a lot of lives and many injured. They say that your Sergeant friend could be getting a Victoria Cross. 'Ow about that, lad!'

Even if Tommy had heard these last words, which he didn't as his mind drifted to an image of the last time he saw his friend a couple of months before, he no doubt would have reflected on what Wally's parents, staunch Christian pacifists, would have thought of their son been awarded the British Army's highest battlefield gallantry award.

The good hearted, gossipy Sergeant Dann was about to continue when suddenly Tommy sat down on the floor and put his hands over his face and began to sob.

The embarrassed sergeant did not know where to look but quickly realised that the soldier before him was mourning a close friend. Unfortunately for the sergeant it was not the first time he had seen such a scene. He patted Tommy on the shoulder and walked away to leave him in his grief.

As the rain grew heavier so Tommy's sobs grew stronger and stronger as all the miseries he had been trying to keep in flooded back into his mind.

Tommy instinctively reached inside the top pocket of his tunic and took out his little carved angel; he looked at the figurine and remembered the time his friend Wally had 'rescued' it from the mine after that deadly explosion in the Hillthorpe pit that seemed now so many years ago. The same Wally who had tended his wounds and helped him to the surface and into the arms of his 'beloved Ma'.

He lifted up the little angel a few inches from his eyes before offering a little prayer for Wally. Tears once more welled up in him, and as it rained the water poured on to the little angel and for a moment it too appeared as if it were weeping, just like Tommy, at all the pain and agony that only death can bring.

As Tommy sat there clutching his precious 'charm' and praying for the end to all this grief he felt only despair; in his anguish the disconsolate soldier felt that nobody was listening to his pleas – especially any loving and protective higher power.

It was then, looking down towards the ground, he saw a pair of boots in front of him and he felt a big hand touch his shoulder. He lifted his head to see who the brown leather boots belonged to and as he did so he saw Siegfried's face – full of compassion, understanding and fraternal love for his suffering English 'kamerad'.

He too knew the loss of a close friend in this ghastly 'Krieg'.

Siegfried bent down onto his haunches so he could look the sitting Tommy in the eye. As he did so he took out something from his trench coat pocket.

'The family photograph,' thought Tommy.

No, there was no photograph. But there instead, in front of Tommy, was unmistakably, if slightly rounder in face and with a larger set of wings, another little carved angel made of pine.

'Santa Barbara, ya?' said Siegfried with a smile, and as Tommy looked up in wonderment, he heard the German utter something like 'Meine Mutter und Vater gab es für mich.'

'Yes,' Tommy nodded, 'Saint Barbara,' and they held up their little carved angels, and the Englishman wiped away his tears and they both laughed.

# Chapter Twenty-three

The time came, however, when the digging was done and the army no longer wanted the services of the lad from the North Yorkshire pits. Just like a piece of coal that Tommy had hacked from a Hillthorpe seam, the British Empire had seen the best of this burned out soldier after he had been thrown on the insatiable fires of the battlefield.

Tommy returned to England and was granted an honourable discharge, a railway pass, a few pounds and a suit – the reward for giving the best years of his youth. He ended up on a railway platform in York, confused and not knowing where he was going. A sympathetic stationmaster found him a waiting room bench to sleep on before putting him on the Durham train early the next morning.

Tommy's confusion arose because, although he wanted more than anything to return to his family, he was afraid of what his beloved Ma would say. Even though he was no longer the seventeen-year-old boy who left that November afternoon to enlist in 1915, he still felt the pangs of guilt in disobeying his Ma – which were so terrible that he had not even returned home after his basic training or on any precious leave during his years of service. For some reason he could never even muster the courage to open the letters sent by his family – in fear that either Ma's loving words or her wrath would push him 'over the top'. What he didn't read could not hurt him, he reasoned.

When Tommy finally did pluck up the courage to return to Hillthorpe he could sense straight away that something was not quite right. He didn't expect a hero's welcome, why should he? At least he had the choice of returning home – not like Bert!

The Collier's Arms, the grocers, the post office and the rows of little mining family houses were just as he had last remembered them. Physically everything was as it always was, but in the air there lay an intangible cloud of sadness. Hillthorpe, like many a village throughout the land, may not have been on the front line, but the lives of its inhabitants were shattered forever in some way – every family, high or low, felt the pain of loss from battles in lands and seas far away.

He turned down the street and there it was – the little two up, two down that Tommy used to dream of when lying trembling with cold and fear in his battlefield trench. Although it was a humble abode, just like any other in his neighbourhood, to Tommy it was the most beautiful place in the world. But the joy of seeing his boyhood home turned to a sense of foreboding; somehow the little house looked even smaller and so much more tired than when he left it.

The stooped figure of Mrs Brown, dressed in black in remembrance of her son George, who had drowned, 'along with all hands', when a battlecruiser had been sunk in the North Sea by a German submarine, swept the steps of number 17. Tommy recognised her at once; she had always said a cheery hello to him when he was a boy and she and Ma were good friends. She looked startled, tried to smile and managed a 'hello, pet'. But her face grimaced as she turned away to hide the tears and continued to sweep the pristine doorstep. Suddenly a chill ran down Tommy's spine and any excitement he had of returning home to his family now turned to a dreadful anticipation. His whole being ached to see his Ma and his family again – oh why, why had he ever left?

138

All his fears were justified when a young woman answered the door when he knocked. It was Emma – not the wee girl he had left behind but one who had grown and filled out into the body of a young woman; her familiar flow of red hair down to her hips and her pretty button nose the give away that here stood before him was his adorable 'little sis'. But as he looked into her loving eyes he could detect a great sadness had pierced her spirit and enveloped her whole being. No longer was she the little Emma he knew; she threw her arms around him, her emotions torn between the joy of seeing her beloved, eldest brother cruelly dampened by the dreadful news that she was about to tell him.

'Oh Tommy, Tommy,' she implored, 'why didn't you write, it's been so long?' As soon as she forced the words out the tears started to well in her eyes.

In the next hour, as they sat at the kitchen table, it all came out. Emma held her brother's hand, giving him comfort as she told of the tragic events that had befallen their family while Tommy was away serving King and Country.

Pa had died within a year of Tommy enlisting – suffering a slow, painful death, brought about by the hacking cough that had tortured his coal-dust filled lungs for the previous twelve years. He was just forty-seven.

There was more tragic news to befall Tommy.

Ma too had died; aged by Da's death she was in no fit health to fight off the Spanish influenza which had swept across the North East in the winter of 1919 and claimed more lives than any war. Emma thoughtfully omitted to tell Tommy that their mum also suffered a broken heart the day her eldest son had left to enlist.

Victor had also joined up, eager to follow his big brother, but he had died too – not on the Western Front, but knocked down by a tram outside a London railway station on his way to Dover.

Only Edward was left – making a living down the pits. He too was a victim of the war, as the bitterness of the last few years had left him finding his solace in drink, even though he was married to Elsie from the sorting shed and they already had two bairns to support. They all lived in the same house, although thankfully Emma was by herself when Tommy walked in the door.

Now Ma had died Emma was the 'mistress' of the house and she looked forward so much to seeing her brother back; for someone so young she had to cope with more than she deserved in her life, but the sight of Tommy and having to tell him of the cruel destruction of their family was too much for her to bear. Her emotions, kept prisoner within for so long, erupted like water bursting through a dam and tears flowed down her cheeks – although she valiantly tried to block the breach, the power of the outburst was too powerful to contain. Tommy, seeing his sister in distress, grabbed her up in his arms as she wept as he hugged her; for a few timeless moments they shared their mutual heartache until they both retreated to compose themselves.

Tommy loved his sister and even more so now that they were united in their common grief; he felt more protective of her and realised that any hurt he showed would merely compound her own. The scrap of a girl he had left behind nearly four years ago had, despite her sadness, blossomed into a fine young woman and Tommy knew that somehow she would survive her ordeal; her kind heart and disposition to care for those around her was a blessing to all those with whom she she came into contact – she was so like her Ma, he thought.

Reality of life in Hillthorpe in 1919 dictated that Tommy find a job right away. This was easier said than done – demand for coal was slack with no more need to feed the insatiable appetite of the monstrous furnaces of the war machine – this, coupled with a mild winter, further undermined the demand for coal and further stoked the numbers of unemployed miners. Besides, thought Tommy, he had no heart to go back to the pit – his life could never return to what he had been, too much had changed it forever.

Like many men of his generation who had been to war, Tommy came back a different man. On the surface much remained the same; physically, if anything, he had filled out and lost some of his boyish looks. But to those who had known him there was something different, mainly in his temperament. In the months following his return to Hillthorpe those who knew him noticed that when they looked into Tommy's eyes it was as if somebody else was 'at home' – not the 'big, daft lad' they had known before he took the King's shilling.

He had always been a big lad, a little clumsy in his movements perhaps, as Bert used always to jokingly remind him, but his outward appearance belied a great sadness within. Tommy had lost his innocent belief that life was for ever. In France he soon learned how cruel and short it could be and how expendable men were – rank and file alike. No mortar shell, no machine-gun bullet, no bayonet discriminated between landed gentry, lowly office clerk or unemployed farm hand – death embraced all, no matter whose uniform they wore.

'Why Tommy, why didn't you come back when you joined up? It broke Ma's heart. She didn't blame you, she understood, but leaving like that tore her in two. Ma loved you so much Tom,' lamented Emma, who couldn't hold back what she felt. 'Yer had no right, Tommy, no right.'

Tommy sank to his knees and put his head on his sister's pinny tied around her waist. 'I know, I know,' he blubbed. 'I'm sorry, I'm sorry.'

Then he did what Emma had never seen her big brother do before. He cried. Tears streamed down the side of his face and he sobbed, before it all became too much for him and he slumped on the floor in a foetal position. From deep within emanated these deep primeval sounds – a noise that sent a shiver through Emma, who stood looking down upon her beloved brother and was frozen by such a heart rending sight.

As Tommy staggered around the room, not fully in control of his physical movements, the tears continued to roll. They were tears of guilt; tears for leaving his beloved Ma; tears for Da and his brothers and Emma; tears for not writing home because he was afraid that Ma couldn't forgive him; tears for betraying her loving trust and for leaving them without a real breadwinner. For what? For King, for country, for civic duty? No, none of these. He realised he been led like a sheep to slaughter – caught up in a wave of sentimental, self-righteous patriotism which swept the nation and sent him, and hundreds of thousands of others, flocking to the fields of Flanders and Northern France to be spiked on its barbed wire and left to rot. Worse still, he thought, unlike so many, he was 'destined' to survive the carnage.

He had taken part in a war he never asked for and one which he knew hardly anything about. Before he enlisted, all he knew was his life in Hillthorpe – Ma and Da, little Emma, his brothers Victor and Edward and his best mate Bert; now, just a few years later, only his sister and Edward were alive, and their lives shattered before they had even begun.

Oh, how he would love to see Ma come through that door, just like she had thousands of times before – with a loving smile and a bag of groceries. If only. But now she never would and it was all his fault!

In his despair he stayed on his knees on the bare wooden flooring board and rocked to and fro – just like he did after the German shell exploded in his forward trench on that fateful day when Bert was killed. He rocked and groaned, and rocked again, locked into another world where no human being should be allowed to venture. Emma fell to her knees and put her arms around her brother, cradling him and willing to share his pain if only he would let her. All the horror of the past few years flashed before Tommy's eyes, and though his mind had tried so hard to cope with the mental anguish his body was now having its voice. As if time stood still, the two siblings stayed until the sobbings reluctantly ebbed away and Tommy fell onto the floor and into a deep sleep.

Emma, who had been so patient and so caring, even when her stiff knees and arms pleaded for movement, rose up to her feet and went in search of something to provide her sleeping Tommy some measure of comfort while he rested his exhausted body. She soon returned, and raising Tommy's heavy head, she carefully placed the pillow under it before covering his body with a woollen blanket.

She kissed him on his temple and whispered 'God bless, Tom' before she was about to leave him to fight the next internal battle as sleep gave him his only sanctuary from his earthly torment.

As she did so, Emma noticed his big left fist, which he held tightly clenched to his chest, slowly open as the slumber began to increase its hold on his shattered mind and body. She saw his strong fingers slowly unfold their grip on whatever Tommy had clung on to with such desperation in his paralysis of despair.

Suddenly Emma's eyes lit up with utter astonishment and joy, for it was as if her heart had stood still and she had become frozen in time. There before her, dropped to the floor, was the little carved angel – the pine figurine – as beautiful and shiny and majestic as that very day that Da and Ma had presented it to her big brother in front of her and Victor and Edward, what was now such a long, long time ago, on her eleventh birthday.

'Oh Tommy,' she gasped. 'Our angel, our beautiful angel. You kept it with you all this time.'

Emma bent down and, with reverence, picked up the angel and her eyes welled up with tears – but this time with joy and relief and hope.

'Saint Barbara was watching over you, Tommy. She protected you – just like Ma and me said she would.'

Emma held up the carved angel and stared at it with admiration.

'I don't know what the future holds,' she said, half to herself and half to Tommy asleep on the floor, 'but you're going to get through this, our Tom. We all are. You'll see.'

Having spoken the words, she kissed the pine figurine, whispered to it a 'thank you' and looked down at her brother with a compassionate and loving smile.

# Chapter Twenty-four

Whatever Emma thought, Tommy knew he was far from 'all right' – his mental anguish continued – and despite his sister's pleadings, Tommy left his home village a few days later. He told her it was for the best. No way could he live in his childhood home, the place where so many memories of the family were enshrined within its walls.

Emma begged him to stay, even arguing that it was 'what Ma would have wanted'. But to no avail. Tommy, although frail in his mind, knew he could not stay in a place where he felt so much guilt. There was no job for him and in his present mental state he knew he could not return to his old job down a pit; he would be a burden to the other men and he still had enough pride to make sure that didn't happen.

Besides, he still had nightmares, waking up in uncontrollable panics, screaming at the ghastly visions of a battlefield he could never escape. No, it was not fair to the rest of them crowded into the little terraced house – not to Emma, to Edward and Elsie, and especially to his little nephew and niece.

Whatever Emma said Tommy could not shed himself of the guilt that he alone had brought disaster onto his family by virtue of his reckless decision to enlist against his parents' wishes.

He hugged a tearful Emma and thanked her for her love and support, but he had to go, and when she asked when would he be back, he simply said something he had learned during his time in France and bade her 'au revoir'. After kissing her affectionately on the top of her head he picked up his kitbag and walked away from the only home he knew.

g

# Chapter Twenty-five

Where he was going he did not know, and for the next few months the former sapper roamed the towns and countryside of North Yorkshire and County Durham.

That winter of 1919 was a bleak one in the North of England; frost permeated every surface, coating the landscape with a glistening, white covering, made even more chilling with bitter and ruthless north-easterly winds.

It was weather where man and beast, if they had any choice, remained inside and huddled beside a fire; but for some, who had nowhere to call their home – however humble – they were at the mercy of the cruel and unforgiving elements.

For forty days Tommy roamed aimlessly around the towns and villages of the North Riding; putting his head down where he could, when only merciful sleep would bring brief respite from his mental torment. He ate where he could, queuing up with scores of other men outside any place which offered some free food and drink or a bed for the night. Tommy was not alone; there were many men like him wandering around with no purpose, just existing for the moment. These men, too, were ex-veterans of the Somme, Ypres, Passchendaele, Arras – scarred for life by their bitter experiences, each one with a horror to tell but nobody to tell it to. Those who had never been to the front, who stayed at home, could never understand their plight and those who had did not want to be reminded of their stolen innocence.

Of course, not every demobbed soldier led such a wretched existence. There were many men who had wives and children or sweethearts to go back to, jobs to return to, careers to pursue.

These were the more fortunate ones who could focus on their responsibilities or pursue new paths to put the last three or four years on the Western Front out of their minds and concentrate on the present and the future. However, even these luckier souls, no matter from what social background they came from, whether rich or poor, who had faced a German bayonet and heard the pitiful cries of the abandoned dying men lying alone in No Man's Land, or stood next to a comrade who had his head severed from his torso by a piece of shrapnel, would never escape the memories of man's inhumanity to man.

For Tommy, the present came with its own fears; how to escape the waves of mental torment and images that he could never erase from his mind. Not even simple pleasures such as the sweet sounds of innocent laughter from children playing in the street, the thrill of hearing a dawn chorus of birds waking from their slumber, or even the warmth of sun beating on his face, could distract him from his constant torture. The heaviness of his load only served to sap his physical and mental strength, spiralling him down into the abyss even further.

Wherever he wandered he recognised so many men just like him, with that far away, vacant expression of the damned. He was caught between living in the present, thinking of the past and despairing of the future. In all the hamlets, villages and towns that Tommy arrived at, it didn't take him long to recognise a kindred spirit – and as soon as he did he just went in the opposite direction.

Every man had his own personal tragic story to tell, but what they all had in common was that they each had a new battle to fight on two fronts – trying to come to terms with the guilt of the

147

survivor, when all around their friends and brothers were either dead or their bodies maimed for life; then, of course, trying to make any sense of it all and finding a reason to carry on living.

The very society that encouraged them to sign up for 'God, King and Country' in the heady days of 1914 and 1915, appealing to a 'sense of patriotic duty', now seemed embarrassed by the very existence of these thousands of broken soldiers.

Where was the 'Home fit for Heroes' they were promised on their return? Where were the spoils of war for those who answered the call of the bugle? Who wanted them now – especially the broken ones?

The last thing that Tommy wanted was to be around fellow ex-soldiers; but he did not have much choice as there were plenty of young men drifting the countryside, just like him. Some took to drink, some became violent; others in their mounting desperation turned to crime; but there were many like Tommy, who stayed in the shadows and kept themselves to themselves, just ignored or moved on by the local authorities, keen that they would soon become someone else's problem.

Tommy slept where he could – in park bandstands, beneath canal archways, on railway platforms, in unlocked barns – anywhere to rest his weary head. The smart suit he was demobbed in, the army trench coat and the standard issue army boots he wore were rapidly falling apart – just like their owner.

To add to his miseries he began to develop a niggling cough that just would not go away. It soon tended to get worse late at night, when Tommy was curled up in any dank corner that happened to be his 'bed' for the night.

Tommy ate and drank whenever the scant opportunity arose – at least the British Army had taught him how to exist on the most meagre of rations. Now his only sustenance depended on the kindness of strangers, soup kitchens, or church charity – and that only compounded his sense of hopelessness and desperation. All Tommy wanted to do was be left alone. He did not want to share his demons with anybody, because that meant that he had to recall, yet again, the anguish and misery of his time in the trenches.

Where he was going to, what his future held, he did not know.

# Chapter Twenty-six

As the rain lashed against his face and the force of the wind made every step doubly difficult across the moorland path, Tommy shuffled, with head bowed, in the direction of the next town. His body cried out for sustenance and warmth and its owner knew not where or when he would be able to satisfy these demands.

The enveloping darkness was another element conspiring to test Tommy's resolve – every step was a challenge conquered; but how much longer could he carry on like this, he thought to himself?

'God, please help me,' pleaded Tommy to his inner being, but 'God,' he continued to reason, 'wasn't listening' and was certainly not going to be present in this bleak wilderness. Tommy considered the consequences of his plight and a wave of black thoughts washed over him.

'I can't go on like this, what's the point of carrying on? Why am I here? I should have died with Bert and all the other lads in the Norkies. At least I would be at peace now.'

To add to his misery Tommy tripped over a loose rock and fell on the pathway in a mighty clump; his face hit something sharp and he immediately felt a sting followed by a trickle of blood slithering down from his temple to his right cheek. The wet of the sodden ground soon saturated through his ragged garments, penetrating through to send a fresh shock-wave of chill to his very core.

As he lay there in despair, and not knowing whether he had any more physical strength left to draw upon, he somehow lifted himself to his knees and his eye caught the glow of a fire in the near distance.

Although aching from pain, inside and out, the flickering light and its promise of warmth and sanctuary, raised simultaneously both his spirits and his body towards the fire. He crawled and staggered forward and, as the glow became larger, his senses began to return; his eyes made out the iridescent flames, his ears received the crack of the burning embers, while, more seductively, his nose picked up the whiff of roasting meat. Tommy moved in closer, transfixed by the magical flames until he was no more than thirty yards from its source. His awakened senses began to hear the distinctive noises of human voices and, as he cautiously approached the light, he made out a small group of people gathered around the large camp fire.

He hid behind a nearby rock, anxious not to be discovered, as he was not sure what reception awaited him if he revealed his presence.

Tommy must have been there a few minutes, taking in the scene of a raucous group of five men and two women. They passed around some bottles, where one took a quick swig before it was grabbed out of his hand by the next impatient imbiber. One man, who looked a little heavier than the rest, stood nearest to the fire and with a wooden spoon in hand stirred the contents of a rounded iron pot, which was suspended over the flames. Tommy, seduced by the smells of the cooking meat, wondered if the gathering would let him join in their moonlight feast.

Driven by his deep hunger, Tommy was just about to rise to declare himself to the gathering when he was jerked suddenly to his feet, grabbed by the scruff of his collar and lifted violently; taken by complete surprise he twisted around but could not

151

escape the grasp of his assailant; he managed to turn to see a thick-set, rough looking man, whom he quickly gauged had a threatening cudgel in his meaty fists.

Tommy tried to elude the grasp of his captor. The thick-set man responded by thrusting the blunt end of the cudgel hard into Tommy's stomach, causing him to wince in pain and gasp for air to replace the breath that had been knocked out of him.

Those crowded around the fire turned to see the disturbance. One of them, a ferret-faced man of scrawny build, called out, 'What you got there Jacko?'

Jacko, still holding his prize tenaciously by the collar, dragged his trophy forward to show off, yanking his captive towards the fire to parade before everybody. Tommy, realising these men were more foe than friend, briefly raised his face to take in the scene. Before him he saw a motley set of dirty, sneering faces, grinning with delight at their new guest's predicament. Tommy, though fearful of the situation, thought that at least he was now feeling the welcoming effects of the heat of the fire.

'This bonnie lad been spyin' on us,' exclaimed Jacko, who took the opportunity to make the most of the group's collective attention, something he seldom enjoyed.

'Must be a police nark, and you know what we do with narks,' spat Jacko who, to emphasise his point, clipped Tommy's ankles so his charge fell crashing to the ground in a heap – much to the amusement of the fireside crowd.

The ferret-faced man, who by a quirk of circumstance was named Ferris, offered his shard of wisdom.

'Awey, man, look at 'im. What nark would walk across the moor on a nite like this? Look at the state of 'im. Mind you, there'll be no rich pickings from 'is pockets. Better tell Corps.'

'You tell 'im youself,' snarled Jacko. 'Don't tell me what to do, you little runt.'

To emphasise his point he glared at Ferris and moved threateningly toward him. Ferris, no match for Jacko in any physical encounter, knew he was on sticky ground.

'Well somebody's got to tell the Corps,' he whined, trying, in vain, not only to justify his comments to himself but also to the rest of the fireside congregation; he decided to make a tactical withdraw away from Jacko's menacing advance.

'I only want some food and water,' offered Tommy, but his plea only met with a slap across his face from the back of Jacko's hand.

'Shut it, nark,' hissed Jacko. 'Nobody said you could speak.'

Two women, both aged in their mid forties, observed Tommy, though in reality they were both in their early thirties, then dived on him, much to the amusement of the gathering. The two went straight for his pockets, both coat and trousers, meeting little resistance from the helpless victim.

' 'Ee ain't got nothin',' screeched one crow.

'Wouldn't get nowt for those rags,' her fellow hag chipped in.

With that, all initial interest on their guest quickly evaporated and the 'party' returned to arguing over who had the next swig of the rapidly diminishing bottles being consumed.

Tommy lay there too weak to respond. Any hope of escape seemed futile – he had no strength to resist and where was there to run? The only real focus of his attention was the rich smell of stewed meat emanating from the large pot swinging above the fire in the wind.

The drunken hubbub of the revellers was once again silenced when Ferris returned with another man. From a distance Tommy could see he was just slightly taller than the ferret-faced man but this one strutted with an arrogance.

' 'Ere he is, Corps; 'ere's the one I was tellin' you about. Don't 'ave much about him, if you ask me,' offered Ferris.

'Nobody did!' growled Corps, not happy to be disturbed from whatever task he was doing. 'Let's see the drowned rat then, Jacko,' he commanded.

Jacko immediately obeyed and grabbed Tommy's hair and raised his head up for Corp's inspection, as if he had served it on a platter.

Despite the blood stain caked on the unwelcome guest's face and the pathetic figure that lay before him, Corps instantly recognised who the head belonged to.

'Well, well, well, what have we got 'ere lads?' mocked Corps, whose face contorted with a malevolent grin. His eyes, which Tommy saw were ignited by the reflection of the flames, seemed to take on an extra shine from the relish of the chance meeting of the man set before him.

'If it isn't my friend, Sapper 'Looney' Wagstaff,' spoken with an extra stress on the 'Looney'.

'Still diggin' then, Wagstaff,' snarled Corps. 'Well you've dug yourself into a right hole 'ere, 'aven't you, boy.'

With that he laughed out loud and his mocking tones were soon accompanied by his acolytes in a choral cacophony of mischievous delight.

'No, lads. Fair game. He's one of us. Served his country in France, fought the Hun and served King and Country. Just like us brave boys.'

Murmurs of appreciation surfaced from the men in the mob, each individual reflecting on his personal bitter experience of his time in khaki. Of course, what 'Corps' had not mentioned was that not one of them could claim to have had an 'honourable service'. Between them their army careers had included incidents of petty theft, bullying, deception, cowardice and misappropriation of army property; two of the malevolents were charged with rape of French citizens, although nothing was proven after witnesses mysteriously retracted on their previous statements. All these 'incidents' were irrelevant now as each justified to themselves that as survivors they had 'done their duty'. What was relevant was they had served and 'did their bit'.

'Course,' continued Corps holding court, 'he was a bloody useless soldier!' Much to the merriment of the assembly. 'Couldn't tell the difference between a shovel and a carbine.'

Tommy's spirits, already low from his lack of sustenance and the threatening surroundings in which he had unwittingly found

155

himself in, now descended to a new abyss at the sight of Corporal Tilsley's face, which was lording over him. It was one that had appeared in many of his recurrent nightmares. His deep contempt for 'this excuse of a man' was his first reaction but Tommy, sensing the danger of the situation, hastily suppressed any visible demonstration towards his despised former NCO.

'You ought to know, corporal, you trained us,' spluttered Tommy, without any irony in his voice and just about audible as he was still trying to get his wind fully back from Jacko's blow.

Jacko, Ferris and the rest of the motley crew smirked and chuckled collectively, amused at the response which, fortunately for Tommy, went completely over the Corps' understanding.

Tilsley looked around, mystified at the merriment at his expense, not quite sure of why that was. 'It was not the first time Tilsley had been in that predicament,' thought Tommy.

'Yer survived, didn't you!' growled Tilsley, 'that's down to my training.'

Convinced he now had re-established the upper hand once again, he continued, 'Welcome to our little company, Wagstaff.' He then raised his voice and walked in front of the ranks for theatrical emphasis: 'The finest regiment ever called to muster by the British Army.'

With this there was a big cheer among the gang.

'I might not be an educated man, Wagstaff, but I think it was old Hook Nose himself, the Duke of Wellington. . .'

'God bless him,' interrupted Ferris.

All, except Tommy, knew exactly what was coming next from the Corps, as they had all heard him say it on many an occasion.

The Corps continued: 'The Duke of Wellington himself said the British soldiers under his command were 'the scum of the earth. . .'

'So meet the scum of the earth,' chorused the rest in unison, before they all fell in a state of convulsive laughter, amused by this familiar phrase quoted by their leader.

'Give him some of yer mush,' commanded the Corps to the cook, 'and a swig to drink. Then get him some rags.'

156

'Thank you,' responded Tommy, who immediately reproached himself for showing such gratitude to a man he truly hated with a vengeance.

'Oh, don't thank me, Wagstaff. Believe me, you'll pay for it,' sneered Tilsley, and with that the cocky ex-corporal spun on his heels to leave the mob for more comfortable quarters, more befitting to a man of his rank. He grabbed the wrist of one of the women and pulled her forcibly towards an outbuilding – much to the annoyance of the other hag who knew her 'friend' at least had the use of a mattress that night.

# Chapter Twenty-seven

It was the smell of the farmyard stench that first awoke Tommy the next morning, that and the piercing cold. He instinctively pulled the thin, woollen blanket over his shivering body. When he finally came to, Tommy began to recall the happenings of the previous night and he temporarily brightened with the fact that he at least had a roof over his head – something he had not had for two weeks – and some food in his belly. It could have been worse!

Then the face of Corporal Tilsley came back to him and the reality of his situation began to sink in. He looked around and saw his campsite companions still sprawled in various positions, under scant covers and bedded on straw; some of the men and one of the women were snoring loudly.

Now fully awake, Tommy's first instinct was to leave his 'hosts' before they too returned to the land of the living. He staggered to his feet, throwing the blanket off his shoulders and began to lift himself from the filthy flagstone floor. Several strands of straw fell off his rising body and he brushed himself down. Tommy turned his attention to the barn door and moved gingerly towards the exit; careful not to stir the others.

'Not leaving already, boy,' he heard a voice from behind him.

Tommy felt a heavy hand on his left shoulder. He turned and there was Jacko, with a wide grin on his cragged face, his smile revealing a few missing teeth – no doubt removed involuntarily by his many physical encounters. 'It wasn't the prettiest sight he had experienced first thing in the morning,' thought Tommy.

'Ain't our company good enough for you, nark?' said Jacko, who at the same time made sure Tommy saw the trusty cudgel gripped in his right hand. Just at that moment the Corps himself appeared inside the barn door.

'Get up you lazy scum. All of you. There's work to be done and that includes you Wagstaff.'

Tilsley approached and put his face a few inches from Tommy's and looked him straight in the eye.

'Course, as you know by our previous acquaintance, Mr Wagstaff, I'm a fair man and now you've been introduced to our humble abode and been shown our hospitality, I assume you will be volunteering to join our merry gang?'

Tommy rocked back to give himself some personal space.

'I'll be on my way now, if you please, Mr Tilsley,' he replied. 'Thank you for the food and shelter.'

Tilsley responded with a malevolent grin, one instantly recognisable by the man standing in from of him.

'Oh, I don't think so, do you, Wagstaff?' hissed Tilsley, again coming forward and staring at Tommy from inches away. 'Not until you've paid your lodging, boy.'

That morning breakfast was prepared by Big Mac, the gang's appointed cook of Scottish descent, and who, Tommy observed, was happiest with a knife in his hand, whether he was cooking or not.

Big Mac did not say much but just handed Tommy a dollop of porridge served in a dirty mug, along with a small chunk of stale bread. Tommy eagerly tucked in and kept his head down, trying not to draw attention. Big Mac went back to cleaning his knife with a cloth and then sharpened it with a pumice stone – a bit too lovingly thought Tommy, who had seen men lavish similar attention on a bayonet in the trenches.

Tommy was just digging, with his finger, the last lick of porridge from his dirty, enamel cup when he received a painful kick in the side of his leg.

'Get up, sapper,' barked Tilsley. Tommy obeyed without comment and scurried to his feet.

'This is Mr Cross, Wagstaff. He owns this farm and he has kindly agreed to give our little itinerant army a place of temporary refuge for some work around his place. It's potato planting season and Mr Cross has employed the services of our select band.'

Tommy looked across at Mr Cross, who was in his mid fifties and by the look of his face, aptly named. Of middle build, Mr Cross was bald on the top with greying hair on the sides. He had a ruddy complexion, which was not surprising for a farmer but this looked, observed Tommy, one that more likely came from too much liking for the whisky bottle.

A bachelor farmer, Mr Cross had inherited the farm as an only child and knew simply the life of a mixed farmer. He had kept it fairly successful for years but now the farm had been reduced to little more than a glorified smallholding – selling off more and more land to pay his increasing debts. Isolated on the moors with little human contact – apart from the rare passing of a farming salesman – Mr Cross was not helped by his increasing liking for the 'odd tipple'. So with potato planting time he was easily persuaded by Tilsley that his 'workforce' could be of some benefit in the short-term. Since their arrival Mr Cross had seen little evidence of this 'workforce' but once he had accepted Tilsley's offer he had little choice but to accept their tenure.

He soon learnt to his bitter cost to regret his pact.

'Can he work?' grunted the farmer. 'Don't look if he has much in 'im.'

'He wuz bloody useless as a soldier,' retorted Tilsley. 'But he's cheap.'

This was a characteristic admired by Mr Cross and for the next few hours Tommy found himself in the 'front garden'.

'Yer likes diggin' don't ye, Tommy lad,' mocked Tilsley, slapping him on the back and handing him a shovel while laughing to himself.

Mr Cross called it a garden, although it was in the same state of neglect as the rest of the farm; a goat and a couple of bad-tempered geese roamed where they pleased.

He handed Tommy a pick and shovel. Tilsley and the rest of the gang smirked before going off back to Big Mac to enjoy the rest of their breakfast.

'Get on with it lad. This is my vegetable patch and I want ye to sort it out. No slackin'. I don't pay ye for slackin', warned Mr Cross, although he did not exactly make clear the 'pay' he had in mind.

Tommy dug, and although his body was still weak from the recent ravages it had endured from the time he had left Emma's loving care, it soon returned to a familiar rhythm and it was not long before he began to make progress on Mr Cross's vegetable patch.

Just before noon Cross and Tilsley returned to inspect Tommy's morning's work.

'By 'eck, 'ee can dig,' acclaimed Cross, who lifted his cap and scratched his bald pate in admiration. 'The lad's done more in a morning than the rest of your men have done in a week.'

'He's been trained well,' replied Tilsley, annoyed that Wagstaff had elicited any appreciation in any form, especially at his expense.

Turning to Tommy, he commanded, 'Put that shovel down and come with me, Wagstaff. We have more important work to do.'

Tommy followed Tilsley to the farmyard where two horses, not in the best of condition he noted, were harnessed to an old wagon. Ferris and Jacko were already waiting and aboard.

'Get on,' ordered Tilsley, who climbed into the driver's seat to take the reins.

'Gee up,' and he tugged the reins sharply, stirring the gentle horses into action as their 'bit' bit sharply into their mouths.

Tommy settled in the wagon opposite Ferris and Jacko, who looked at him with distain.

'Where we going?' asked Tommy.

'Shut it nark, you'll find out soon enough,' growled Jacko.

The light drizzle and fresh breeze did little to soothe Tommy but he was used to such transportation from his army days; the jolt of the wagon on the uneven road and the rough surface of the wooden carriage against his back and legs, only added to his general discomfort.

'Still,' he thought, 'it beats walkin'!'

After about three miles the travellers came to the village of Arksborough and Tilsley brought the wagon to a halt with another violent tug of the reins. Tommy looked out and observed a metal sign fixed on top of a wooden post flapping in the wind. It was badly in need of a lick of paint, thought Tommy, who took in the pub sign of a bushy tailed animal caught in a man-trap. Tommy read the lettering underneath – 'The Fox and Snare'.

The occupants alighted from the wagon and Tilsley, Jacko and Ferris gleefully entered the front door of the public house.

'Line 'em up, Arthur,' instructed Tilsley to the man behind the bar, who was obviously the landlord. The moustached man, smoking a cigarette, did not seem duly surprised at their abrupt entrance.

Tommy took in his surroundings and it definitely did not have the welcome feel of the Collier's Arms, where he and Bert might sneak a pint if their Das were not watching.

Apart from two old men hogging their pints and crouched over a game of dominoes, accompanied by two mangy greyhounds at their feet, he noticed there were no other customers. The furnishings were tatty and it was not the cleanest of establishments.

Arthur, clearly in no rush, stubbed the end of his Woodbine into an ashtray already three quarters full of extinguished cigarette butt ends, and began to pour the first of four pints of porter.

'I'll just 'ave water,' said Tommy. 'That'll do me.'

162

'You drink what you're given,' snapped Tilsley. 'Now sit down and shut up.' He turned to the landlord. 'Come on Arthur, we could die of thirst waiting for you.'

Arthur took no notice and continued in the same slovenly fashion until he finally 'lined 'em up' on the bar.

'That'll be one and fourpence,' offering out his hand in anticipation.

'Put it on my slate, Arthur,' responded Tilsley, who glared back at the landlord, not without a little hidden threat.

Arthur knew he would have a long wait for that slate to be wiped. He grunted and withdrew his outstretched hand. Good job he had other means of income apart from the monies he took over his bar – as Tilsley knew perfectly well.

Tilsley picked up his pint and took a gulp before slamming another full glass in front of Tommy, who was sat at the table.

'Drink,' he ordered.

Tommy thought resistance was useless and besides he did have a thirst.

'Now then Wagstaff, I'm going to give you a chance, being you and me are old muckers in the Norkies. 'Ow would you like to join us, eh? You ain't going nowhere, lad. You can't even put food in your belly or a roof over you head.

'Now, I'm willin' to let bygones be bygones. I can find a place for a big lad like you – come and work for me and you'll never be hungry again. What do you say, Tommy?'

Tommy looked at Tilsley and his former NCO almost had a benevolent and sympathetic smile on his face – something he had never seen before.

Tommy gulped a mouthful of porter, giving him a little time to swallow Tilsley's proposition.

'I'd rather not. I'll take my chances, if it's all right by you,' came the reply.

His reply brought a sharp change in Tilsley's features and his face reddened to portend the rise of his infamous temper.

'Why, you ungrateful little shite,' exploded Tilsley. 'Too

good for us, he is, eh lads.' Tilsley addressed Jacko and Ferris.

The pair, who had already swiftly downed their pints, whetted their lips – this time in anticipation of an act of violence from their leader that they both thought was surely imminent – or perhaps it could have been for the next glass of porter.

Just at that point the sound of an engine rumbled outside the pub and a lorry came to a halt before its driver turned off the ignition. Tilsley was just about to smash his near empty glass over Tommy's head, knowing Jacko already had his trusty cosh in hand ready if Tommy had offered any resistance.

But fortunately for Tommy, the moment was broken when a tall, thin man in a shiny, three piece suit made his entrance.

'Come on Corps, where's my pint? And while you're at it I'll 'ave me Irish too,' chirped the confident newcomer.

'Phelan, about bloody time. You got the stuff?' said Tilsley, who quickly changed his persona and now switched his attention to the more elegant man.

'You got the money?' was the reply. 'Anyways, you can't get anything until I've had my pint and dram.'

Tilsley nodded to Arthur. Arthur took his time.

'Right, let's not beat about the bush, Phelan. How much?' queried Tilsley, whose temper had evaporated now business had to be done.

'To you,' said Phelan in his charming Irish lilt, 'We'll call it twelve pounds, and you'll be robbin' me.'

'You can't be robbing someone who never paid for it in the first place,' retorted Tilsley, who surprised himself with his ready wit. 'Call it ten pounds.'

'Ten guineas and ye have me spit,' offered Phelan with a well practised smile, offering out his hand to shake.

'Ten pounds,' said Tilsley, 'my final offer.'

'Ten guineas it is then,' continued Phelan with hand still outstretched.

Tilsley spat on his hand and took Phelan's to seal the deal. Both grinned awkwardly, each happy with their bargain.

164

Tilsley gave a wad of banknotes to Phelan and the two smiled warily at each other.

'Line em' up again, Arthur,' bellowed Tilsley. 'This time they'll be on our Mick friend,' said Tilsley, pleased to have the final word on the transaction.

Tommy, not used to the alcohol, was feeling its effects but savvy enough to keep his head down for the moment and out of range of Tilsley's eye.

When Arthur finally had all the glasses arranged in a row on the bar Phelan took his and raised the tumbler to the heavens.

'To business,' he boomed.

'To business,' echoed Tilsley as he and Phelan clinked each other's glasses.

Jacko and Ferris grabbed their pints – leaving one on the bar intended for Tommy.

'He won't be needing that,' opined Ferris, 'he ain't one of us, is 'ee? Seems such a waste to leave it,' referring to the full glass of porter.

Ferris went to pick it up but Tilsley glared at him and Ferris withdrew his hand. Tilsley snatched the pint and plonked it heavily on the table in front of Tommy, spilling some of the contents.

'Drink it,' commanded Tilsley.

Tommy, observing Jacko reaching for his little metal friend, wrapped his fingers reluctantly around the glass and began to drink.

'Sup it up in one, boy. I've got a job for you right now,' snarled Tilsley, not forgetting the perceived slight Tommy had given him a few moments earlier.

Tommy wearily downed the murky fluid, cheered on by a grinning Jacko and Ferris, and once finished he was grabbed by the arm tightly by Tilsley and led outside. Phelan followed, as did Jacko and Ferris.

Phelan lifted up the canvas tied to the tailgate of the truck and inside the flatbed was full of heavy bags.

'Told you so,' triumphed Phelan. 'Two tons of the finest fertiliser, do any farmer proud. If anyone asks you, you can honestly say it fell off the back of a lorry.'

Phelan and the two henchman appreciated the humour but Tilsley decided to ignore it.

'Now then Wagstaff, get loading and look lively,' ordered Tilsley, as if directing a raw recruit on the parade ground.

'Stick it in the wagon and don't spill nothing' or I'll spill you,' he warned.

'Come on, lads,' Tilsley addressed the other three men, 'time for a quick pint. Though nothing's quick as far as Arthur's concerned,' laughing to himself, and soon joined by his compatriots who were eager for another spot of lubrication.

The four went cheerily inside, heartened also by the fact that it had now started to rain heavily – helping to make their 'guest's' task even more unpleasant. They sat at the window watching Tommy go about his onerous work, goading and smirking at his efforts. By the time Tommy had finished his task it had taken the gang another two rounds to guzzle down and put on the slate.

When Tommy's work had passed Tilsley's inspection, the latter gave Jacko and Ferris instructions to climb into the now heavily laden wagon – Jacko to share the front with Tilsley and Ferris to climb on top of the fertiliser bags.

'Wait there a sec, Corps,' chirped Ferris, with a bit too much enthusiasm for Tilsley's liking.

With that Ferris scurried down the side of the pub and came back less than a minute later rolling a wooden barrel, obviously taken without the consent of the landlord.

'Thirsty work, loading lorries, Corps,' said Ferris, a sentiment that both Tilsley and Jacko had no objections with.

'Get it in the back of the wagon,' ordered Tilsley, for some reason anxious to return to the comforts of Cross Farm.

Jacko and Ferris lifted up the barrel between them and then slid it over a bag of fertiliser or two to disguise their newly acquired property.

166

'You an animal lover, Wagstaff?' asked Tilsley, who after a few pints of porter was even more nasty than ever.

'Yes, of course,' answered a bewildered Tommy. 'Why?'

'I thought you were,' mocked Tilsley. 'You can't expect those poor beasts to bear all this weight, can ye boy. Which is why you have to walk.' With that he burst into laughter at his own wit, swiftly followed by appreciative howls by his fellow gang members.

Tilsley jumped into the driver's seat, tugged the reins hard and took up a whip before cracking it at each of the horses' rears for emphasis. The two distressed animals whinnied in protest, which brought a further crack of the whip from Tilsley – this had the desired effect on the horses, and the cart and its cargo slowly gathered momentum.

Tommy trudged behind, not helped by his intake of alcohol fuelling his emaciated body and being bowed by the now driving rain. Ferris kept a beady eye from on high, making sure that their reluctant recruit did not go 'AWOL'.

167

# Chapter Twenty-eight

Three long and sodden miles later and they were all back at Cross Farm, greeted by the owner himself, Big Mac, and the two female camp followers.

'Well,' he said to Tilsley, 'did you get it?'

'Yeah, all there. Now give us twenty quid,' demanded Tilsley.

'How much?' queried Cross with an inflection of surprise.

'Twenty quid, you heard. You can't complain, you've got a bargain. Now hand it over,' commanded Tilsley.

Smelling the alcohol and Tilsley's breath, the farmer realised it was useless to argue and reluctantly handed over the money.

Tommy, glad to be back 'home' at the farm, almost fell with exhaustion as he staggered to the nearest low wall to find a welcome seat, glad of the opportunity to recuperate.

Jacko and Ferris eagerly lifted a bag of fertiliser between them and pulled the barrel of beer down to take to their quarters, arguing among themselves who was its 'owner'.

'What the hell do you think you're doing, you lazy tyke,' bellowed Tilsley as soon as he saw Tommy had sat down. 'You can do that when you're finished unloading it into the barn. Now get to it!'

Tilsley enjoyed the moment as did his acolytes.

'Come on lads, it's tea time, ain't it, Mr Cross,' as the assembled party headed across the courtyard to the shelter of the farmhouse, leaving Tommy to his labours.

That evening Tommy lay on his bed of straw in the barn, resting his weary limbs from the digging and lifting of the day.

He heard the creak of the barn door and instinctively rose to his feet in case of trouble, a wise step as around the corner came his despised corporal, not a little unsteady on his feet with a beer bottle in his hand.

'You think you're better than me, don't you Wagstaff?' scowled Tilsley. 'Think because you keep to the straight and narrow you can look down yer nose at me, don't you. Well let me tell you boy, you're a bloody fool.'

Tilsley, though a good six inches shorter than Tommy, squared up to him, provocatively staring him in the eyes. Tommy could not but help inhale the distasteful stench of alcohol from Tilsley's breath which was mixed with an odour of cheap tobacco.

'Wagstaff, you're nothin' but a bloody fool. You play by the rules and you get nowhere in life. War to end all wars – bullshit,' and Tilsley spat on the floor to emphasise his disgust.

'The only ones who gain are those who started it in the first place. The rich, the gentry, the landowners, the factory and mine owners, the politicians – when the war is over they just grab what's left and share the spoils out and start all over again.

'You and I, Wagstaff, we're cannon fodder and that's what we'll be in the future, mark my words. Homes fit for heroes. Pah!' and he spat aimlessly on the floor again.

'No homes, no jobs and no bloody hope, if you ask me! You believe all that crap, about King, God and Country. The King, Kaiser and the Tsar, they were supposed to be one big royal family, protectors of the nations, and they're little family quarrel has ended up with millions dead.

'And where's this God supposed to be when some poor bastard is bleeding and screamin' like a pig on barbed wires or is lookin' scared and helpless as a German storm trooper rips a bayonet out

h

of his stomach?

'If this war has taught me anything, boy, it's that you got to look after number one, cuz nobody else will. If you ain't got it, Wagstaff, you got to bloody well take it, cuz that's exactly what those big knobs and their ancestors did. They just grabbed it and didn't let go.'

With these words Tilsley suddenly became aware that his sermon was falling on stony ground.

'Come with me, boy,' ordered Tilsley and he grabbed Tommy by the collar and dragged him forcibly out of the barn to a small outbuilding nearby.

Tilsley, in his drunken stupor, eventually located a key after searching most of his pockets, and when he did find it unlocked the padlocked door. He opened it and pushed Tommy inside.

Tommy was amazed at the sight held before him. The whole room was a collection of silver candelabra, oil paintings, silver trays, grandfather clocks, antique furniture and other treasures. Tilsley opened a chest of drawers from a well made Welsh dresser and showed off its contents of various bits of jewellery and silver plated knives, forks and spoons.

'This, Wagstaff, is my spoils of war, as I call it. It's something that me and the boys have been collecting on our travels – our 'Grand Tour' they may say in more sophisticated circles.

'Now Tommy, I'm showing this to you because, take a look,' and with that Tilsley proudly waved his hand to convince his reluctant guest. 'I'm showing you cuz part of this could be yours. Join us lad, and me, Jacko, Ferris, Big Mac and you will want for nothing.'

Unexpectedly, to Tommy, Tilsley put an arm around him as if he was his best pal.

'Soon we'll be going south. I've got contacts and I'll get a good price for all this, and there's more to come wherever we go. Come on Tommy, what do you say?'

'Thou shalt not steal,' Tommy said, rapidly concluding that these were 'ill gotten treasures' before him. 'That's what it says in the Bible and that's what Ma taught me.'

Those words wiped off any amiability that Tilsley had pretended towards Tommy shortly beforehand and sent him into an instant rage.

'You ungrateful little shite,' he hissed, and with that he picked up a nearby candelabra and took a swipe at Tommy with considerable force. Tommy instinctively moved away but not before a weighty, glancing blow had knocked the side of his head and upper shoulder. He crumpled to the floor in the doorway of the outbuilding. Tilsley dragged him out into the courtyard, padlocked the door, put his key in his pocket and walked away, leaving his victim to his fate.

Soon after, a groggy Tommy crawled and half stumbled back to the barn to take refuge. In the early hours of next morning Tommy left Cross Farm, aided by the heavy sleeping of the rest of the residents who had finished off the contents of the stolen beer barrel.

Once more Tommy ambled down the road, knowing not where he was headed. This time, though, he had food in his belly and his thirst quenched, but his body still had to cope with a very sore shoulder and a raging headache.

# Chapter Twenty-nine

One March day in 1920 Tommy found himself in Swaledale, not knowing how he had really got there or even recalling where he had spent the night before.

It was market day, when the rural town was alive with the sounds and smells of a large number of people and animals confined in a small area, in a place which had been home to such a rural tradition for hundreds of years. Even though the rain poured steadily, there was an air of expectation as buyers and sellers alike hoped that the day, for some, would harvest rich profits and, for many, the chance to catch up with fellow farmers and friends, old and new.

With the country on its knees, after the war had sapped its economy and the North Riding was especially hit with the closure of many of the pits, the markets still thrived although there was scant money around. No matter how bad the economic situation people still had to eat, food had to be produced and sheep, cattle and pigs, brought to market. The local market attracted hordes to Swaledale, drawn by the multitude of stalls that had sprung up overnight in the square, the thriving trade at the livestock centre and, of course, the long opening hours of the many taverns, which enjoyed an extended licence for the day's proceedings.

For Tommy, who wandered the market like a lost sheep and was not used to all the bustle of human activity, the noise and frenzy began to overpower him in his fragile state.

After more than six weeks of living rough and the lack of proper sustenance to feed his stomach Tommy's mind and body began to rebel. As he staggered around, like a Friday night drunk, through the wide and lively streets of Swaledale, all he heard was the acerbic comments of strangers, eager to get out of the path of this obviously penniless itinerant.

'Get away from my stall,' shouted a middle-aged owner of a vegetable stall. 'We don't want your sort round 'ere,' he barked.

A young woman, aged in her twenties and dressed in fine, fashionable clothes, topped by a petty, yellow bonnet with a burned orange sash tied around it, held her hand to her nose as Tommy approached her.

As he passed, Tommy heard her say to her female companion and deliberately loud enough for him and those in near proximity to hear: 'Look at the state of him, they shouldn't let that sort of people roam our streets – he's obviously drunk.'

Tommy began to cough and the woman scampered hurriedly away, afraid of catching whatever ailment the tramp was blatantly suffering from.

He spotted a communal horse trough for the animals to refresh themselves and bent down to scoop some water to drink; after gratefully satisfying his thirst he ladled the fresh, cold liquid between his hands and washed his face and beneath the top of his shirt to wipe away the dirt from his neck and at the same time rub some life into his weary body.

Again Tommy coughed and this time he felt a deep rack of pain emanating from inside his ribs.

Three men, aged in their middle twenties and who were loafing idly around, doing nothing in particular, and resting their backs on the sides of a farm cart, began to snigger.

'Aweh lad,' jeered one, 'I don't want my horse down with something nasty. He's worth a few bob.'

'At least your horse is down wind of him,' sneered another, and all three burst out laughing at Tommy, who did his best to ignore their cruel and unsympathetic remarks.

The coldness of the water and the rapidity of him digesting it triggered a strong reaction in Tommy's stomach; a wave of nausea hit him hard and he broke out in a shiver and sweat; all of a sudden, without warning, he began to retch all over the side of the cart.

'Oh, the dirty bastard,' screamed one of the trio of idlers, 'he's thrown up all over my cart.'

The man, who made up with muscle what he lacked in height, grabbed hold of Tommy, spun him around and in one movement flung him against a barrow of apples that was next to a fruit stall. Tommy immediately felt a crack on his skull as his head collided with the wooden casket and a sting of pain as his arm scraped along the rough, cobbled street floor.

The stall holder, who at the time was serving a customer and who had not witnessed the bruiser tossing the unsuspecting Tommy into his barrel, turned around swiftly when he heard the sound of the casket being knocked to the ground and saw its contents scatter all over the street.

He looked at Tommy, who was now writhing in a curled up foetal position, moaning with terror as if some whizz-bang had suddenly exploded above his head; the stall holder then took one look at the bruiser who had perpetrated the assault and immediately decided, in his own best interests, that it must have been Tommy's fault for the loss of his precious stock – especially when the bruiser provided a menacing glare at him to sweep away any doubts he may have had of who really was to blame.

'You dirty beggar,' cried the stallholder. 'Look what you've done, you'll pay for this, my lad,' before he himself began to kick a defenceless Tommy in his back and ribs.

This fresh assault was very much to the amusement of the bruiser and his two stooges, who laughed and mocked at the hapless stranger crawling in pain on the floor, with his hands protecting his head.

To add to the injury, a number of boys, no more than eleven or twelve years of age, picked up the loose apples and started hurling them at the unfortunate figure on the ground – before tucking a few of the pieces of fruit into their trouser pockets.

At the scene of this public 'crucifixion' a sizeable crowd began to form – noisily joining the rising cacophony of jeers and mockery. The more they laughed the more the bruiser and the stall holder were encouraged to bait poor Tommy. The victim wailed with an almost inhuman cry, scared and confused – not just because of the physical pain his body was enduring but cowered by the unsolicited attention of a baying crowd and what seemed to Tommy a hundred or more pairs of hateful eyes.

Just as the bruiser punched again the defenceless Tommy sprawled helplessly on the ground, the crowd parted when a tall, blond haired man stormed fearlessly through their vicious ranks.

He stood more than six feet and had the build of a light heavyweight and those in the crowd instinctively knew that he was not the sort of man 'to mess with'.

The bruiser was just about to deliver his final blow to Tommy and did not see the newly arrived entrant closing rapidly in on him. As the bruiser raised his clenched fist, the blond man grabbed his arm to prevent the pummelling to Tommy's head; in one swift motion the blond man spun the bruiser around to line him up before punching him with a meaty fist right on the bridge of his nose; the bruiser, as if hit by a sledgehammer, fell five feet backwards at a rate of knots and crashed right through the main display of the fruiterer's stall – much to the consternation of its owner.

'What about my fruit,' he wailed, 'whose going to pay for it?' The blond man turned to raise his fist again, and the fruit stall man decided – having again quickly reassessed the situation – not to pursue the matter any further.

The gallant rescuer, without any fear that the bruiser would ever get up again to continue the altercation, now turned to the crowd.

'You've seen enough, now move it,' he shouted, and the crowd dispersed like a flock of sheep before a snarling collie, their entertainment for the day definitely over.

'You two there, don't just stand gawping,' said the blond man pointing to two male bystanders, 'give me a hand with the poor bugger, for mercy's sake.'

As the two men put their arms under Tommy's armpits to raise him to his feet, the blond man looked into his face, which had blood pouring down from an open cut.

'Eh lad, it's you, isn't it? Sapper Wagstaff. My God!' exclaimed the taken aback blond man.

Tommy lifted his head, which was still an effort as he tried to gather his senses, and slowly began to focus on the face of his 'knight in shining armour'.

There was no doubt who it was, Tommy recognised him instantly, and even in his semi-conscious state he managed the beginnings of a smile as he was still trying to recover from his unwarranted beating.

'Sarge,' he croaked. 'Is that you?'

'Not sergeant now, Wagstaff, just plain Mr Howie,' grinned Ted as he nodded to the two men holding Tommy to let him try and stand on his own feet.

It was just like the time, thought Tommy, when Sgt Howie and the two soldiers had picked him up on that awful day three years ago in the trenches when Bert was killed.

Trying to stand by himself was too much for Tommy and he began to cough loudly, and winced as he protectively held one of his broken ribs.

'Come on Wagstaff, let's get you straightened out,' said Ted. 'You look as if you've been in a war.' Ted's face broke out with a mild grin, when he realised the irony of his last comment.

'Alright lads, take him to Doctor Fitzgerald, there's a pint each in it for you. Tell the good doctor I'll be down shortly and I'll square up with him later.'

One of the men raised his cap. 'Yes sir,' he said and the two men put their arms under Tommy's armpits again and proceeded to drag him in the direction of the town's only surgery.

# Chapter Thirty

For a month Tommy remained as a guest at the home of Ted Howie and his wife Irene.

She was a kindly, understanding woman, who had heard and seen enough from her husband to sympathise with a former soldier; be it a stranger, who was recently returned from the horrors of war. Irene was a shrewd woman and although her husband had come back in one piece – thank God – she too knew that the experiences he had endured had brought back a man different from the one she kissed off at Darlington station, what now seemed such a long, long time ago.

Ted was now the assistant works' manager for Swaledale Town Council, a job he was quickly promoted to on his return, unlike the previous incumbent whose body, or parts, remained somewhere unknown – deep beneath the battered countryside of a Flanders field.

During his time with the Howies Tommy was rested, cleaned up and fed and watered – mainly due to Irene's diligent care and her plain, but ample cooking. His ribs were beginning to heal, the hacking cough disappeared and no longer did he suffer from the dizzy spells that dogged him in his emaciated state when he was a 'gentleman of the road'.

Tommy stayed in the spare room of the Howies' three-bedroomed, semi-detached Edwardian townhouse, and enjoyed the simple pleasures of a comfortable bed and a roof over his head for the first real time since he left his old home in Hillthorpe to sign up for 'King and Country'.

However, despite the 'luxury' of such care and compassion by his two new friends, as Tommy lay in bed at night his old nightmares soon returned, unrelenting, like a wave of German infantry attacking a British front line.

Many a night he woke up, eyes bulging, sweating and screaming with fear, as the faces of the dead paraded past him in his mind. Ted and Irene, sleeping the other side of Tommy's bedroom wall, could not help but be woken themselves, more nights than they cared to remember.

Despite the screams from the room next door they both understood their new lodger's plight and when Tommy, once again, came down for breakfast after yet another restless night to apologise for his 'outburst' Ted and Irene just smiled and quickly changed the subject.

'Now then, Tom,' declared Ted, 'have you thought of where you are going to go and what you are going to do? You'll always be welcome here lad, you know that. But now that Irene's soon to be having a bairn, we have got to look to the future.'

It was true, and all the evidence Tommy needed was Irene's bulging stomach, which had expanded rapidly since he was first taken in by the Howies.

'Now, I know you find it hard Tom, but you can't go out roamin' again, drifting, you have to find a job,' said Ted. 'I know your body's up to it, you've a good pair of shoulders, a strong back and good heart but, well...' he looked at his shoes as he hesitated to tell what was unfortunately the truth... 'The thing is, nobody is going to employ you Tommy, with your mind not quite right. It's not your fault, lad, it's just the way it is.'

Tommy stood silent, and he too looked down at his shoes. He knew his friend was right and respected and took on board anything that Ted Howie had to say. He just nodded in agreement.

'Look Tom, I'm lucky. I'm fortunate to have employment, a good job with a steady income, and if times were a little different I could offer you a job as a labourer with the council, but the budget is tight at the moment – there are no jobs.'

Tommy looked up at Ted and nodded his understanding.

'I know, Ted,' he said. 'I thank you and Irene for everything you've done. I'll be alright, you'll see. I'll be on my way soon.'

There was the trace of a film of water in Tommy's eyes but he fought any sign of sentiment, although this didn't fool Ted, an experienced man when it came to dealing with men and their emotions.

Ted placed a hand on Tommy's shoulder. 'Don't worry lad, I'll think of something, that's what sergeants do. If we left it for the officers to work out, nothing would get done,' he said, with a well practised, wry smile on his face.

Two weeks later Ted came back to the house with a big grin on his face and Irene was already suspicious.

'There must be something up,' she thought, 'if Ted looks that happy!'

'Irene, Tommy,' Ted barked as if addressing a cadre of raw recruits on parade, 'I've got some good news. I've been in contact with Reverend Collins at St Anthony's in Yeasley. His last gravedigger,' and he dropped his voice a little, 'just say, he's in need of one of the plots himself at the moment.'

After the slight embarrassment of the circumstances concerning the vacancy, Ted continued. 'Well, put it this way. He needs a new assistant sexton now; the money ain't much but it's regular and there is a one room board at a church cottage in the grounds. I told him about you, Tommy, and Reverend Collins said he's willing to give you a trial. It's perfect for you Tom, you like digging, don't ye lad?'

'Aye,' said Tommy, as he nodded in agreement at Ted and Irene. 'I like digging.'

# Chapter Thirty-one

*April 4, 1920:*

'Right Tommy,' said Mr Parkman, the verger of St Anthony the Abbot's Church, 'I want you to dig plot 334 down by the lychgate. The vicar has booked in a burial service there for 2.15pm. I would start now if I were you lad, looks like it's going to pour down later. Sooner you start the better.'

'Aye, Mr Parkman, I'll get diggin' right away,' Tommy replied.

Claude Parkman looked at his clipboard and reminded himself of the name of the departed soul whose body was due to be the latest recipient of a resting place in St Anthony's graveyard.

' 'Ere, Tommy,' he proclaimed, as if he was addressing a congregation from a pulpit, an ambition he clearly had. 'You might know this old soldier. Says 'ere 'e wuz in the Norkies.'

Tommy lifted his head in response.

'You wuz in the Norkies, weren't ye, lad?' enquired the verger.

The gravedigger nodded his head in reply.

'Let's see,' continued Mr Parkman, 'e wuz only 25. Name's Tilsley.'

Tommy could not believe his ears.

'What's his name, Mr Parkman?' asked the younger man, needing time to get over the shock of the news delivered to him and wanting to make sure that he had heard right.

'Corporal Archibald Tilsley, King's Own North Yorkshire Volunteers,' confirmed the verger before continuing, 'Did ye know 'im lad?'

'Aye. . . ' mumbled Tommy, in a state of shock; he hesitated before repeating himself, although still a little confused. 'Aye.'

'Well Tommy, it must be satisfying for you to know that yer helpin' bury an old comrade of yours; one of your own,' consoled the verger, before rubbing his chin with the tip of his pen, demonstrating that he was deep in thought in the matter.

Tommy offered no further information about Archie Tilsley and even if he was asked to he would have remained silent.

'Speak no ill of the dead,' was a phrase that came to his mind.

But Claude Parkman had not finished his ruminations.

'You know, Tommy, I think I read about this lad Tilsley in last week's Yeasley Gazette.'

It 'just so happened' that he had the newspaper tucked away in his coat pocket; he intended to go into the vestry to catch up with the news later while Tommy laboured on plot 334.

He took out the local Gazette and flicked through until he reached page five. Mr Parkman began to refresh his memory following an earlier peek at the paper.

He continued: 'Yes. . . I remember, now,' as he scratched his chin a bit more as if to reveal some profound revelation, '. . .it said 'e was a war 'ero who served his country in our 'our of need. Just like you Tommy, eh? Though you ended up in the Pioneers Corp, didn't yer lad? Not that you didn't do your bit. Course you did. I just remember Mr Howie saying you were in the Norkies like.'

Tommy did not respond but this did not deter the inquisitive verger.

'I would 'ave done my bit, lad, you know that but I was married and a bit too old for the first call to arms. . . They wouldn't let me leave the jam factory, couldn't run the place without me they said. I was under foreman at Tyke's Preserves

182

but everybody knew who the real boss was. We did our bit for the war effort at Tyke's. An army marches on its stomach. You know that Tommy. I bet you 'ad some of our jam at the front didn't ye lad?'

But Tommy's thoughts had, respectfully, long drifted away from Claude Parkman's war record.

'You said Tilsley, Mr Parkman?' he asked, more interested in returning to the fate of his despised former corporal.

'Oh aye, Tilsley,' said the verger, now returning to give his version of the report in the *Yeasley Gazette*.

'He was murdered,' announced Mr Parkman in dramatic tone, with an emphasis on the word 'murdered'. The verger glanced at Tommy to see his reaction – there was none.

'Sez 'ere he was killed in a pub brawl at the Fox and Snare public house near Swaledale. Tilsley was a respectable businessman in the second hand goods trade but got knifed by one of his "associates" in a drunken argument over the share of the profits.'

Continuing to read from the paper Mr Parkman added that Tilsley was murdered by 'one Willy McDonaghue from Prestonpans in Scotland or "Big Mac" as he was known in the criminal fraternity.'

Tommy gave no hint that he knew the murderer and his victim.

'Poor sod,' opined Mr Parkman. 'This Tilsley chap, volunteers to do his duty, fights at the Somme and is a 'ero, survives the rotten war, does all that only to get himself stabbed to death by some big loony while enjoying a drink in a country pub. It makes you think, don't it, Tommy?'

But Tommy's mind returned to the night Big Mac sat by the campfire sharpening his knife with obvious relish, and a cold shiver went down his spine at the thought.

'Well Tommy,' said the verger in an authoritative voice. 'Yer can't stand around 'ere talking all day, you've got a grave to dig, lad. Best get on with it.'

` With that Claude Parkman swung around his not inconsiderate bulk and made his way to the vestry for a cup of tea with the *Yeasley Gazette* in hand and his clipboard tucked underneath his armpit.

'Aye, Mr Parkman, sir, it will be done,' said Tommy, touching his cap before heading towards the tool shed as the raindrops began to fall from the heavens.

# Chapter Thirty-two

At plot 334 Tommy stood erect and deep in thought. The rain fell heavily that Tuesday morning in early April and there was a brisk, north-easterly wind cutting through the hills and the churchyard of St Anthony the Abbot.

It was now a well practised ritual with Tommy; before he began his labour he stood and mumbled a little prayer in honour of the recently departed who was soon to occupy the latest, freshly dug grave. Every person that Tommy buried – rich or poor, young or old – was important to him – each an individual and most of them loved and valued by someone – and to the digger from Hillthorpe, even if they had no one to mourn them, they were all loved by their Lord and saviour, Jesus Christ.

'Even Archie Tilsley!' he murmured to himself.

After a short period of respectful silence, Tommy picked up his well worn shovel and began his labour. No longer did he have to mark out a grave, his eye and experience knew exactly how long, how wide and how deep to dig.

A film of sweat soon touched Tommy's brow as he settled into a rhythm of shovelling the rich Northern soil.

'I like digging,' thought Tommy, and it was not long before the shape of the grave soon became defined and, as he wedged the

j

earth onto the flat of the pan, not even the fierce drizzle and biting wind could distract the steely Yorkshireman from his humble task.

The clouds darkened, gathering like a flock of Wensleydale sheep to the whistle of its shepherd and barked into its pen in the sky by his obedient and faithful Collie dogs. Tommy's perspiration was now diluted with a salty wash of rain that permeated through his work overalls, but the digger hardly noticed. No, as he rearranged the grass, mud and stone of his beloved Yorkshire countryside the gravedigger at St Anthony's was no longer aware of the physical reality around him. The deeper he dug, the deeper he lost himself in thought back to the many victims, who were once his comrades, on a field near to the River Somme.

Rainfall began to invade his freshly dug grave but Tommy continued his arduous task.

'No "splash" of rain is going to come between me and my work,' he thought, 'this is nothing compared to the flooded trenches; there's not even any gunfire or the reek of cordite in the air.'

He just kept digging. As he laboured, back came the faces of those who died in his regiment, and it was not long before the face of Bert dominated his thoughts – the face he remembered as his pal crawled towards him from the forward picket – just before Corporal Tilsley made his fateful appearance.

All the horror of his wartime experiences flashed before him; the twisted limbs, the stink of foetid body fluid, the rotten corpses – all fragranced with the distinctive, sweet smell of death. The 'flower of a generation' whose corpses once belonged to young men, who before their tragic end, were just like millions of others of their generation, full of vigour, passion and hope for the future.

As the rain increased its severity, water permeated its way through Tommy's boots and mud began to ooze its way into the bottom of his trouser legs and onto his socks; his hands, as solid and hewn as tree stumps, were both numb with cold and dripping with rainwater but nothing could slacken his steady grip on the wooden, ash handled shovel or distract its user from his earthly duties.

With all the skill of a seasoned artisan after years practising his craft, Tommy's mind and body worked in unison, swinging into action. With the edge of the steel blade he cut into the soil, shaping the grave as he went, before patting its sides to leave a flat, even set of walls. He worked in rhythm, a syncopation that was simple in action and effective in result. Trenches and graves, they were all the same to Tommy.

As he took a pause to regain his breath Tommy straightened his back and swept the back of his huge hand across his brow; at that moment, as he levelled his focus on top of the grave, his eyes were caught by a distinctive, familiar lick of red standing out from the drab grey and earthy colours of the graveyard.

Emerging for the first time that Easter season was the bloom of a little poppy flower with its black stamen caped by its red petals. It was only a tiny, shrivelled plant, struggling to emerge from the soil, and awash in a fine coat of rainwater; it looked weather beaten and trampled – no doubt from the boot of a rare visitor, who strayed from the path and had crushed the little bud underfoot in search of a loved one's grave. But to Tommy's eyes the little poppy's vivid colour and defiant presence shone in contrast to all the drabness that surrounded the graveyard.

As he watched, a gust of strong wind caught the petals of the little flower, which doggedly refused to be bowed. Tommy smiled and as the rain dripped down the back of his collar he was suddenly reminded that there was work to be done.

Down he dug, and shovelfuls of earth began to form an increasing pile beside plot 334. The further he descended into the grave the more Tommy reminisced about his days on the Somme front line. The only way he could 'forget' his torment and hellish images was to dig; his occupation and its physical demands were his only distraction, while his limbs were engrossed in labour his corporeal demands took precedence over his tormented mind, bringing a brief solace to his tortured soul.

187

Down he dug; the rain now reinforced with a biting chill, but no elements of nature would prevent Tommy from completing the grave of St Anthony's latest incumbent.

The blade of the shovel bit deep into the earth as Tommy leant to place his weight behind the cutting tool; he scooped a full pan of fresh soil and in one swoop flung it over his shoulder and onto the growing pile at the side of the grave.

As he dug, the faces of the dead came back to haunt him; some he had known at school, many from the pits he had worked in; others he knew from his early army days, where they shared the miseries and joys of the parade ground, the slops of mess food, the draughty bivouacs that were their only shelter from the unforgiving elements; that and the 'love' of a good sergeant major and his obliging NCOs. These were the same men, who only a few months before their debut to war, were wide-eyed boys, with whom Tommy had shared endless square-bashing and needless marches on empty stomachs and bleeding feet. These were the faces he recalled from the months he had spent billeted in inadequate canvas tents, shivering in thin, course blankets, on the merciless, bleak Yorkshire moors for more nights than he cared to remember.

Now these faces were remembered solely today by those who loved or cared for them before their grisly death on foreign fields or as they still appeared etched in the forefront of Tommy's tortured mind. There were so, so many, thought Tommy.

He even remembered the Germans he 'laid to rest' in a mass grave he had once helped to prepare; his job was to 'sprinkle' buckets of lime on them, like holy water, to quell the pungent rottenness of their foetid corpses. As he deposited the contents of the pan over their remains, Tommy thought how their faces – wherever they came from; Germany, Austria, Hungary – to Tommy they looked just the same as his fallen comrades. All the dead soldiers to him faded into one.

The rain continued to pour, the wind gathered momentum but still Tommy dug; this time it was the face of his friend Bert which came before him, the one petrified, frozen in features by his fear as he made his way back to Tommy and the British front line trenches. Tommy's mind focussed on those haunted eyes as Bert gazed for the last time into those of his boyhood pal. It was the look of a drowning man about to go under the waves, holding out a hand in desperation in vain to a powerless onlooker before he sinks for the last time into the murky depths; his was the look of a tortured soul being dragged into the abyss by demons guarding the gates of Hell itself.

The steel of the blade hit the earth with an added vigour and the thud of its impact coincided with the roll of a tear that made its way down Tommy's cheek.

The agony of his thoughts swept over him; it was as if he was hit by a giant tide of misery, completely engulfing body and soul.

'Why not me Lord, why did you not take me instead? Why did you let me live?' he cried to the heavens.

The tears began to flow faster, but the pain still remained; Tommy sank to his knees, dropped his shovel and knelt down deep in the hole; his whole body now began to convulse with sorrow and frustration; his wet, muddy, aching hands now covered his face – as if he was ashamed of venting his emotions; he sobbed and began to rock – just like he did when Bert was blown to pieces and the time he lay in a pathetic heap before his heart-broken sister.

'Please God, no more, no more!' he cried. 'No more!'

It was then he remembered the little carved angel and, despite his sobs, managed to put his hand into his trouser pocket.

He took out the pine figurine and looked at the tiny angel which held out its arms as if to embrace him with its golden, feathered wings.

As Tommy wept, still holding the carved angel but prostrate at the bottom of his sodden, water filled grave, enwrapped in a cloak of wretchedness and despair, he suddenly heard the sound of a child's giggle.

'Oh no,' thought Tommy, 'somebody's coming, they mustn't see me like this.'

Quickly he put the angel back in his pocket and picked up his shovel – anxious not to be caught in such a miserable state.

He retuned to his digging, his body bent as he resumed to attack the soil.

As he did, again he heard the high pitched giggle and he stopped his digging to look up from his pit. Standing before him was a little girl – a pretty little thing, with a mop of fair, curly hair – she couldn't have been more than about four years old, thought a stunned Tommy.

He wiped away any traces of tears, lest she had spotted him crying, and rose to stand erect.

The little girl, whom he did not recognise, held in her hand a small, well worn, but obviously well loved, Teddy bear, which had a button black nose with amber and speckled glass eyes and a coat of dirty brown.

The child smiled warmly at the gravedigger and giggled again; she did not say anything but beckoned him to come with her before once again laughing, spinning around and running gaily off towards the church. Tommy, entranced, suddenly noticed that it was no longer as cold as it was, the rain now began to settle into a light drizzle and there was a glimpse of the sun emerging from behind the clouds.

Compelled by the intriguing, mysterious little girl, Tommy clambered out of the grave to see where she had gone; as he climbed out of the deep pit and began to get to his feet on the ground above the grave, he looked around again to see where she had gone. As he brushed the freshly dug remnants of mud from his clothes he saw the little ball of energy, topped by her mass of curly hair, run and giggle the short distance up the path to the porch of St Anthony's.

She turned a final time, gave Tommy a beautiful smile and beckoned him to follow her. As he did, Tommy felt a great warmth drape over him; he made his way up the gravel path and before him, just about twenty feet away, Tommy saw his little friend join a group of people, one of whom gathered up the beaming child into her arms.

190

As Tommy drew closer, all the people in the group turned to look at him and he suddenly stopped in sheer wonder. He stared in astonishment, firstly at the little girl and then to the woman who carried her. He couldn't believe what he was seeing – it was Ma. Ma!

Ma! She looked so young and beautiful – just like she was when he was not much older than the little girl before him. She smiled at him and his whole being at once rejoiced with happiness.

He couldn't believe it. As he looked again there was Da in his Sunday best, looking so smart and handsome – for the last few years of Da's life Tommy only remembered a bowed, wheezing man who looked far older than his real age; now he glowed with health. Da waved at his son, just like he did when Tommy was a little boy and his father was going off to work in the early hours of the morning, before first light, to begin his shift at the pits. Da would give Tommy his special wave, for him and him only, as Tommy looked out of the bedroom window while his younger brothers and baby sister slept and Ma was working, preparing for the day, downstairs. Tommy returned the wave and felt a pang of joy that his Da was no longer suffering the cruel plight of many a collier.

Tommy then glimpsed two men standing behind Da in a familiar uniform; the distinct khaki of the British Army, with one decorated with the epaulettes of the King's Own North Yorkshire Volunteers.

There was Bert with a big wide grin on his face and 'the cheeky bugger', noted Tommy, even had a pint of bitter in his hand – no doubt from the Collier's Arms, which he raised to his astounded friend, who stood frozen to the spot with his jaw dropped in wonderment.

Next to Bert was another young man – this time a good few inches taller than when he last him, but there was no doubt to Tommy who it was – Victor. Victor gave him a proper full salute, with a grin as wide as the Tees, which a bewildered Tommy could

only return, more by reflex and years of army discipline than by any conscious action, as his limbs were strangely not reacting to his brain's commands – such was his amazement.

My God, there was Wally. Walter Smethick looking as pleased as punch! He had his uniform on and Wally looked directly at Tommy, pointing proudly to the three stripes on his shoulders and laughing.

Behind this beloved band stood a tall figure, unknown, but at the same time, remotely familiar to Tommy. The female had long red, flaming hair and fine leonine features, as if beautifully carved out of the most exquisite alabaster. Her wings, whose span was raised in a protective fold of all those before, were of the most brilliant, pure white, as were her vestments. To Tommy she just seemed to float, head and shoulders above the rest. The angel smiled at Tommy and at once he felt a penetrating surge of love and compassion that he had never before experienced in his life; Tommy stood transfixed and immediately knew that from now on his life would never be the same again. An inner peace at that moment came to replace the angst and turmoil that he had endured over the past few years.

Before, Tommy's restless mind was filled with the horror of dead comrades and foe alike; it was like he had carried the death masks of those who had suffered like a macabre set of frames from a photographer's album. But now, as the angel at the rear of the group stood before him, these images were banished forever – evaporated as fast as the rain which had earlier fallen on the graveyard of St Anthony's the Abbot Church and had now suddenly ceased and been replaced with warm, shining sunlight.

Like the shutter of a camera capturing a precious moment in time, the only image that would now be imprinted in Tommy's mind was that of the wonderful vision of his beloved Ma and Da, of Victor, Bert, Wally and the giggling little girl with her teddy bear – all reaching out with their love.

As he stood there rooted to the spot and enthralled by the sight before him, Tommy beheld the angel – for surely that's what it was – lift her beautiful set of golden wings which engulfed all those before him; a bright light emanating from her being and a translucent glare that so startled Tommy he put his hand up to protect his eyes; when he put it down again the celestial group had all disappeared.

Tommy gasped – panting to return air to his lungs as he tried to come to terms with what he had just witnessed. At that moment a second wave of love hit him with a force which penetrated his whole body and soul. He felt a euphoria which revitalised and refreshed him in a way he had never known, or would again, in his life in this world. It was as if a huge burden had been lifted from him and Tommy knew he would never be the same again.

Time stood still for Tommy as he stood staring at the spot where he had seen his vision. He was still in a daze, not knowing what to do next, but after a few minutes Tommy turned and returned to plot 334 and the completed, freshly dug grave.

Instinctively he again took out the little pine carved angel and stared in awe as he recognised that it was the same one he had witnessed just moments before.

He kissed the little figurine, and smiled again before putting the precious wood carving back into his pocket.

As he bent to pick up his tools and was about to leave, Tommy saw before him the little poppy, stood tall and erect, straining towards the rays of the now warm and sparkling Easter sun.

It was then that Tommy noticed something so breathtaking and beautiful to behold that he knew that what he had just witnessed was not just a vision, but his own personal miracle, meant for him and him alone.

If he had any doubts that he must have been hallucinating or dreaming they were now irrevocably dispelled forever as he took in the spectacle all around him.

After the rains had stopped, the whole of the churchyard and the surrounding area were basked in the full majesty of glorious sunshine. As Tommy walked down the church path with his tools slung over his shoulder, like a Lee Enfield rifle, he took in the wonderful sight. The entire churchyard of St Anthony's was covered by a swathe of distinctive red and black poppies. Poppies proudly stood to attention as if on parade, sprinkled around the graves of those laid to rest in the North Yorkshire earth.

It was the same little flower he first remembered, what to him now seemed a lifetime ago, on a distant French field. That little poppy, by the side of plot 334, was joined by hundreds, if not thousands of its 'comrades in arms' as if saluting the caring gravedigger.

It was Tommy's turn to smile, and as he shut the gate of St Anthony the Abbot for the last time and the latch clicked behind him, he said to himself out loud: 'No more digging for you Tommy, old lad. No more digging.'